Dawn of Unease
An Alexis Chronicles Prequel Novella

J L Park

DAWN OF UNEASE

First edition. July 23, 2019.

ISBN: 978-0-473-48470-5

Written by JL Park.

CHAPTER 1

What would you do if the monsters you thought you were protected from were there with you all along?

The imposing, looming grey walls surrounding GreyBrook were all she had ever known. Towering over the fledgling city, threatening in their size and their power to hold out the horrors of "Outside", the horrors of "Before", they dwarfed anything and everything around them. Gleaming in their silvery newness, the razor wire adorning the very top glinted in the sunlight. It had been said by those who were there in the beginning that the moment the walls were completed, the sense of relief, of protection, was palpable. For a long time, it remained that way.

Until now.

"GREYBROOK CITIZENS!" A loud, but familiar voice sounded over the loudspeakers, a pause following to ensure all citizens were giving their full attention. "It is I, your Illustrious Leader, Ellwood Marshall. It has come to my attention that certain members have complained about treatment within Grey-Brook. Dare they question the laws, the rules of GreyBrook?!" He roared,

Hushed tones swept over the crowd that had gathered around the loudspeaker, surreptitious glances at their neighbour for subtle looks of guilt. Was it them?

"They dare to claim they are treated unfairly in the great city of GreyBrook, within these great walls! The same city and walls that give them shelter and provide them with a way to support their families, away from the negative and disruptive influence of the Outside! Is this NOT enough!? They expect to be able to make accusations of those around them and not being punished!? Is that not what brought the downfall of the Outside!? Is that not what brought Grey-Brook from a dream into a reality, into a necessity!?" Ellwood's voice gained in volume as he spoke, amplified by the loudspeaker until he was almost deafening, driving the crowd into a frenzy.

"Dare they question our laws and remain unharmed? Do they not know the law? 'If one is of the fairer, and weaker sex, certain accesses must be granted - to one's husband, and anyone whom he has given permission to. If one is without one's husband, and one is approached for certain activities by those of male gender, then one must answer in the affirmative. If one does not, it is within the law for the shunned male to take what he wishes, if that is his desire. Without consequence.' It is written into the law that has been laid down since the beginning of this great city of GreyBrook, spoken unto me by Higher Powers than I. Dare they question those Higher Powers?" The women around this loudspeaker moved slowly as one, backing away from those frenzied GreyBrook citizens that they were surrounded by. Subconsciously, they had all managed to aim for the same place, becoming a group. Married women to the outside, able to use the excuse that their husbands had not given permission should they be approached.

The walls were supposed to protect us from the monsters, and yet they were on this side, with us.

"ISABELLA MARIA SCOTT," my mother hissed my full name in my ear, as she tugged on my arm, "Get in here." I allowed myself to move with her, confused, as usually I was ignored.

"Mama?" I murmured, as she pulled me towards the middle of the group.

"You're of age." The panic in her hissed warning matched the concern on her face. I had recently had a birthday. Whilst it was not something, we usually celebrated in GreyBrook, it was acknowledged that I was now of age to be married. I glanced around as she pulled me further, noticing suddenly the looks on the women's faces. They were either terrified for me, or as I discovered, pulling on my arm, trying to draw me to the outside where the frenzied group of men were gathering. Luckily, I wasn't averse to a quick elbow to the face even to those who I respected, or at least had respected.

Reaching the middle, surrounded by others my age from this area, we allowed the group to move as one towards people's homes. Breaking off as people reached the safety of their homes, the group began to diminish. A sob broke free from someone beside me. I glanced sideways, noticing the tears streaming down the face of a girl not much older than me.

"What's wrong?" I murmured, grabbing her with my free arm, Mama still pulling me with the other, her fingers digging into my skin as I tugged her to stop. The girl hiccoughed but walked with us.

"I live in the other direction." She muttered; her eyes wild with panic. I stole a glance at my mother, we were heading in the direction of our house.

She sighed and nodded. "Come with us. The curfew just means you need to be inside by the time of the horn. They've never said where you need to be inside."

I grinned, as I pulled her closer, "You can be my sister for the night." She gave me a grateful smile and allowed herself to be pulled along with the group. Unfortunately for us, we lived at the furthest end of where this group would go. No wonder Mama looked panicked.

"Isa, you have your knife?" She murmured as she slowed slightly, getting as close to me as she could before she spoke, able to feel my head as I nodded, "Good."

"Hey, new sister, what's your name?"

"Meredith," She murmured

"I'm Isabella. Isa for short. You need to grab hold of my mother's other hand; I need mine free. Mama, this is Meredith." I pulled her hand over to my mother's free hand. When I was satisfied that she had grasped hold of Mama's hand, I let go of both of them. Pausing slightly, I reached quickly into my boot, secreting the knife I had hidden in there up my sleeve, before jogging within the thinning crowd to catch up with them again.

"Got it?"

"Sorted, Mama." She nodded, as she looked ahead, preparing herself for breaking off. I glance behind the small group we were in now. The men still following, their group also thinning. Many had only joined to be able to protect their wives from those who didn't have specific permission from them, others were not in this for altruistic means. Thinking of one thing, and one thing only.

I glimpsed the top of my father's head within the crowd and suppressed a smile. I wouldn't have to fight them off for long before he got there.

"HEY! EVERETT! LET ME have a go with ya missus!" Called an unknown voice, followed quickly by the unmistakable noise made by a fist connecting with the soft cartilage of a person's nose, and the grunt of the injured party.

"Fuck off." My father's voice carried from where he was, "She's mine, and only mine." I frowned, as that statement didn't sound like my father. I glanced at Mama, who had a small grin on her face, as she shook her head in that 'It's okay' movement.

"That nice piece of arse, that's your 'of age' daughter then?" That wiped the grin of my mother's face, as she pushed me behind her. There was a primal sounding growl from the direction I had last seen my father in.

"You even think about that and I'll -" he was cut off

"You'll what, Everett? You know we don't actually have to ask your permission? She's not married and is now of age."

Mama glanced back, our house in sight, "Do you think you can get to the house before they can?" She hissed in my ear.

"I think so."

"Knife out. Don't be afraid to use it. And RUN!" She pushed at both me and Meredith, as she stayed back to help hold them away.

WE DIDN'T HAVE TIME to sneak a look behind us, as we heard the roar of several men.

"Faster! It's the last house!" I hissed, breathlessly at Meredith, who seemed dazed. I punched her in the arm to startle her out of the daze she was in, which seemed to help, as she darted past me, barrelling towards the house. I let the knife slip down my sleeve into my hand, as I sprinted after her. This wasn't the first time I'd had to run home, but this time was for my own safety. Meredith stumbled in front of me, barely keeping upright as she ploughed ahead. I was too scared to look back until we were shoving at the door to get it open. A few of the men had managed to get around the thinned-out crowd, and my parents and were not far away, still running. The door finally opened, and I shoved Meredith through, slamming it behind us.

"Geez... that was close," I panted, bent over my knees, trying to catch my breath. Meredith had fallen as I shoved her through the door, so was lying on the floor on her back, panting.

"Does that happen often?" She muttered, trying to catch her breath.

"No, it's not the first time I've had to run home, but the first time they've been after me with a legal right to do what they like if they catch me. I've never run so damn fast in my life."

"Neither," She sat up, eyes warily on the door, expecting them to run through at any moment, jumping as there was a thump.

"Isa!" I jumped, not recognising the voice at the start, "Isa, it's us. Let us in. Quickly!" I heard the urgency in my father's voice. Things must not have gone well. I stood, flicking the lock on the door, as it flew open, my parents falling in the door after it. My father's eyes flicked towards Meredith, then back at me.

"She lives on the other side of town," I started, "Papa, this is Meredith. Meredith, this is my father, Everett." Meredith pulled herself to standing and reached her hand out to shake his.

"Pleased to meet you Meredith, though I wish it was under other circumstances." Shaking her hand, "Do you need to get hold of your parents?" She nodded, "Come with me, I'll get them on the phone." She followed him to the landline we still had. GreyBrook was slowly phasing them out, since Ellwood had discovered that some could still ring outside.

I LEANED OVER AND SLID the knife back into my boot. Mama waited until Meredith had left the room before sighing with relief.

"That was too close, Isabella. Luckily you run fast," She looked worn out, as she continued, "But, we need to be more careful with you from now on."

I sighed, "Has it always been this way Mama?"

"No, Isa. GreyBrook started as a way to continue the old ways without interference from the Outside, when they felt that things were changing too much in the Outside. It was touted as being the best thing since giving women the vote, to the women any way."

"And I gather, it's not. From what I know of it, and what happened today."

"No, it's no longer that. It was okay to start with. I guess I never agreed with the premise of the rules or the city. But your father's family did, and because there was only me and him protecting me," She smiled, hands folding over her belly, "and you inside me, there wasn't anything for me to fight to stay in the Outside for. We would have had no support, so we came into GreyBrook."

"Was it better than this at the beginning?" She had tried to quietly tell me when I was younger, I recalled, but I didn't understand the issues then. I did now.

"It was. Ellwood created GreyBrook as a way to get around the social change happening, where women were standing up for themselves, and powerful men were falling from their long-held positions due to actions that they had made in their pasts or were currently still doing. But in the beginning, it was all about everyone getting along, and creating the rules. We had to work together to make it work, so they had to give thought to what we women had to say."

"Did they?"

"Yeah, they did. But the moment the laws came out, since the first few years here, things have changed. It never used to be as dangerous to be a woman of marrying age. Hell, you didn't have to marry when we first got here. Your father and I weren't, until the laws changed. Then, for your protection as a baby, and my own as a woman of age, we chose to." She looked down, sadness crossing her face, "Little did we know, we could only protect you for so long, and that it would just get worse, not better, in GreyBrook." I reached out to touch her hand,

"You weren't to know, Mama." She shook her head, a sad guilt passing across her eyes.

"Yes, I should have," She said sternly, "But enough of that now. It's the way it is now, and we have to figure out how to keep you and Meredith, safe."

"It's not all of them though, Ma." A small grin crossed her face, as she muttered something that sounded like '#NotAllMen' to herself, a private joke that I didn't understand.

"No, no it's not. It's enough of them, Isa, for your father and I to be concerned." I frowned, I recognised some of the men from earlier as fathers of friends of mine, husbands, not single, hormone crazed boys.

"Neziah's Dad was in that group threatening you and me earlier," She nodded, she'd seen him, "What would make a father, a husband, want to... come after a teenaged girl?" I suddenly grew concerned for Neziah, she was only a few months younger than I was, but our fathers seemed very different.

"I don't know, Isa. Your father doesn't either. He might hang around with the same people and say some things in their presence that aren't his normal style, like earlier. But he doesn't understand overwhelming drive to have sex with anything that happens to be female and of age, just because you have the right to do so without consequence," She allowed herself another smile, "I married a good one there."

I grinned, "Seems like you did! Do I need to worry about Neziah?"

She shook her head, "Not from her father, anyway. She is almost of age, yes?"

"Yes."

"There are laws against fathers doing such things with their daughters, mostly for the genetic issues that any child conceived would be at risk of, than any respect for the daughter," she muttered, her lack of faith in the intent of the law very clear in the tone she used for that one statement, "So, I don't think you have a worry there - Mr Archer is usually a law-abiding citizen. It's just that several laws allow him to come after you or others of your age. She is at the same risk from any other man as you are, once she is of age." I shook my head sadly,

"How do you find one that isn't... sex-crazed?"

She laughed then, slapping her hand over her mouth, "At your age? Most of them are. Always have been though, even on the outside, before GreyBrook. Your father was." I blushed; I didn't need to know that! "But, if you find someone who can respect you, and not push his wishes onto you, even though by law he is entitled to, then he's usually one of the good sort." I smiled, ending the conversation as Meredith and Papa walked back into the room.

"Your parents okay with you staying here?" Papa shook his head, as Meredith did the same.

"No, my father does not want me to have to find my way home tomorrow. He would like to come and fetch me tonight." She allowed a small smile to tickle the corner of her mouth, "He also wants to be able to thank you for keeping me safe during that... whatever that was. He likes to do those kinds of things in person." Papa smiled, patting her shoulder.

"My kind of man. There are a few good ones still in GreyBrook, I promise."

AS MY PARENTS SET ABOUT getting a meal into the oven and waiting for Meredith's father to arrive, we talked quietly at the table. Meredith still seemed a little shaken from the frenzy and the run.

"Does that, whatever that was, happen often here?"

"Not really. Only if Ellwood stirs things up, like he did this afternoon," I frowned, "What do you mean - here? Where in GreyBrook are you from?" She blushed, looking down at her hands, chewing on her lip before she answered.

"Near the Confederate Circle,"

I must have looked shocked, as she looked more ashamed when I didn't answer straight away, "Cripes! That would have been a hell of a walk in the morning!" She looked at me, stunned that I didn't really care that she was from a much fancier area of GreyBrook than the one we lived in, "What the hell were you doing this far out?"

She laughed, "Being nosey, really."

I grinned. I could imagine that for those with a bit of money, influence or both, those of us in the outer limits of the city were a curious bunch. "Picked a day for it then! But to answer your question properly - no, what happened today has only happened a couple of times that I remember. Today was the first time I was in danger though, having 'come of age' a month or so ago. Usually only happens if Ellwood is in a shit-stirring mood, and he seemed to be today,"

The guilt that crossed her face startled me, "Oh... shit. Do you know Ellwood?" I could be in serious trouble. Though, with today, what was new?

"Yeah. But it's okay, I won't tell him! He's my uncle."

I looked at her, incredulous. "Meredith, Meredith Marshall?"

She lowered her eyes as she nodded,

"Ah, shit. Then, I sincerely apologise for speaking with disdain for your uncle and will endeavour not to do so again." I was trying to cover my arse, backtracking even though I meant every word, and every feeling that was behind what I had said. From what I knew of the outside, I'd be full entitled to have spoken that way, but GreyBrook was different.

Seriously different.

CHAPTER 2

Awkward conversation followed. Watching my tongue was not something that came easily to me, particularly not when I actually needed to. Meredith could tell I was uncomfortable and tried to make it easier on me

"Isabella, he's my uncle, not my father. My father doesn't even like him all that much. I'm not going to say anything," she paused, thinking, "and hell, you wanted to know why I came out this way? I wanted to see what the hell he thought he was doing. I couldn't see that his rants were going to go over well in the outskirts, when they've started to ruffle a few feathers in the Confederate Circle. Those who had been ruffled were usually those who would never say a bad word about Uncle Ellwood, even when they should, but I've heard whispers, so I came out to take a look at what it was doing out here."

"It's certainly ruffling feathers out here!"

"Yes, it is. Though, the frenzy those guys got themselves into? That seemed a little weird."

I chuckled, "I suppose it would. That was a once in a blue moon occurrence. They're normally not like that. The thing that disturbed me today was that I knew a few of those doing the shouting. They're in my classes at school," I sighed, "I know the law, I know they have rights, but did they really need the reminder? But now, they're going to be awful at school as well."

Meredith seemed concerned about something. "Closer to the Confederate Circle, we have protection once we come of age. It's almost like Ellwood knows exactly what he is doing, when he whips them up like that, and knows that if he let anything happen to the children of his most close supporters, or his family, that he would lose control of GreyBrook," I frowned, I didn't understand where she was going with this until she continued, "But it seems you don't have that protection out here. Yes, I managed to escape mine this morning to get out here. Father was furious. Isa, have.... you.... They...?" She stumbled over her words, unsure how to ask what she needed to know.

"No, Meredith. Even though the law states I'm not allowed to talk about it if it did happen, it hasn't." I smirked, when she looked at me like she didn't believe me, "I'm mouthy enough I'd talk about it even if I wasn't supposed to, so you can believe me when I say it hasn't! I do know a few people it may have, though."

She nodded, "Thank you for your honesty, and telling me what you think of my uncle, before you knew he was my uncle."

I was about to say something to her, when there was a knock at the front door.

"Ah, Welcome Mr Marshall, please come inside," My father ushered him inside, a car running outside, waiting. Papa had known who Meredith was the moment he laid eyes on her, having his suspicions confirmed when they called her parents.

"Thank you, Mr Scott, - for taking my daughter in, when she is not supposed to be out this far, much less being caught up in the skirmish that occurred this afternoon,"

"You're welcome, Mr Marshall. She was more than welcome to stay if she wished,"

"No, she is outside the Confederate Circle's protection out here, and we need to get her back into the Confederate Circle, where her security detail has been suitably punished for allowing her to slip out without him seeing her. He will be manning her security detail 24hrs a day for the next month as punishment. Where is your daughter's security detail? Or your wife's?" He looked genuinely startled that we had no such thing. That we just went about normal life and hoped for the best.

"We don't have them here, but we manage, usually." Mr Marshall nodded once he had overcome his confusion at the differences between those afforded the luxury of the Confederate Circle, and those of us out in the actual city. Papa and Mr Marshall spoke for a few moments, before Mr Marshall made to leave with Meredith.

A SHARP CRACKLING SOUND startled us all, as the in-home broadcast sprung into life, Ellwood's voice booming through the speaker.

"Citizens, you are all required to present yourselves to the nearest billboard screen to where you will be at 12 noon tomorrow. Any who are not accounted for, and have no excuse to not be there, will be punished. GreyBrook in its entirety must bear witness to the punishment for complaints on unfair treatments in GreyBrook. That is all." It screeched as he ended the broadcast.

I turned to Mr Marshall to gauge a reaction, surprised to see him shaking his head, muttering. A similar surprise was evident on the faces of my parents.

"That idiot brother of mine is going to lose what little grasp of control he has over GreyBrook, if he thinks this will work," Meredith winked at me, as her father looked up at us and realised that we'd heard him, "Oh, did I say that out loud? He's my brother so I can call him an idiot, I have to put up with him." My parents visibly relaxed. I took strange comfort in knowing there was someone in a high position within GreyBrook that seemed normal. What was normal though? GreyBrook certainly wasn't

Meredith gave me a quick hug, thanked my parents for their hospitality, and left with her father.

THE BELL SOUNDED AT exactly noon the following day. The billboards blinking into life with a darkened picture. Grainy outlines of two people could be seen in the murkiness, until spotlights in the area stuttered into life, projecting light onto the two figures that, until then, had been shrouded in darkness. A barely stifled gasp echoed around me, as we took in the fact that these two women had been stripped bare above the waist, and had their hands held above their heads by ropes. A darkened figure moved towards them, their face shielded from the camera by a dark hood, dragging a whip behind them. A hush fell over the crowd as the figure drew their arm back, and struck one of the women across the back, drawing a yelp of pain from them. A sharp red welted line rose quickly over the area she was struck, as the crack of the whip was heard a second time, this time on the back of the other woman.

The pace at which the figure struck was slow, methodical, practiced. Each strike timed at just the right point that it would have felt as though they had stopped striking, the pain startling the women out of the semi-conscious state they appeared to be in. Blood seeped slowly from their wounds as the figure continued. Red rivulets trickling down their backs, the crowd so quiet I was surprised that we couldn't hear the droplets of blood as they hit the sand beneath the woman's feet.

I didn't want to watch, but found I struggled to tear my eyes away from the scene playing out in front of thousands of people around GreyBrook. Guilt at being a witness to this cruelty weighed heavily on my shoulders. Some part of me wanted to know what they had done, what unfairness they had accused someone of, just to stop myself from doing it. I gasped, as I realised Ellwood's plan was exactly what was happening. He wanted us to witness this to ensure we didn't do what these women had done, to ensure we knew our place in the world. I shuddered as I looked up again, the women struggling to remain upright, their knees buckled, backs a mass of blood and open wounds. The figure had stepped away, as Ellwood's face came into view.

"Citizens of GreyBrook - take this as your warning. Should you feel that any treatment you receive within GreyBrook is unjust, or unfair - remember this scene. These two women accused several fine, upstanding men of sexual assault. For taking what is rightfully theirs to take - one is unmarried, and the other the men requested permission from her husband - everything they did was lawful. Complaints about treatment within GreyBrook will be taken seriously. Heed this warning, women, if you do not wish to end up with the same scars these women will bear for life. Curfew is now enforced from 6pm. That is all."

I glanced around as the crowd started to disperse, a sea of shocked, bewildered faces turning back towards their homes or workplaces.

"What the hell did we just witness?" Muttered a young man next to me, a guilty look for speaking ill of anything Ellwood did crossing his face quickly.

"I believe it was a warning to the women, and those who are of age." I muttered, "to suck it up and deal with what the city of GreyBrook dishes out to you."

He shrugged, not convinced, "Still doesn't make... that right."

I smiled at him "No, it doesn't. But don't let Ellwood catch you saying that." He laughed and patted my shoulder as we went our separate ways.

I CAME HOME THAT DAY to find my parents hunched over something on the table. They startled as I spoke.

"Did you go to the billboard?" I asked, I hadn't seen them. My mother looked up, her face pale, but her eyes blazing with an anger that was almost rage.

"Yes. We did." She clipped her words short, her hands trembling. There was an awful lot of rage churning under her attempt at being calm, I was not going to get a good response if I asked any further questions. I knew that tone, that look, but had never seen it this serious. As though she would explode if she said anything other than those clipped words.

I nodded, moving closer to the table, as she tried to lean over it.

"Whatcha doing?" My father glanced at Mama, as though he was checking that it was alright that he said something to me. This was confusing, my parents were rarely angry, and never to the extent of what was simmering under the surface with my mother. Nor did men in GreyBrook ask for permission from their wife to answer a question whose answer contained personal stuff. She nodded curtly, pouring over the sheets of paper I could now see on the table.

"We can't tell you right now, love, just that it MUST be done, and we may need your help."

"I'll need to know more than that to help you out, even if you are my parents. If I'm going to get in trouble for anything, I'd like to know well in advance what I'm likely to get into trouble for."

Mama lost the edge off the rage in her eyes, relaxing slightly "We know that. Not today. We've done enough for today. How are you doing after the... "She rolled her next word around her mouth before speaking, as though it tasted off, "*display* we were witness to today?" Her eyes softened, watching me.

"I felt guilty just watching it, but I realised that was his intent. He made us watch to put us off saying anything. So, I'm confused. Wasn't GreyBrook created intending to make things better? This seems to head towards making them worse." My father smirked and continued cleaning up the stuff they had been pouring over.

"That was the intent, and if you look at it, for SOME of GreyBrook everything is better. Just not for us."

"What do you mean it's better for some?"

My father piped up then to answer my blurted question, "Look at it this way. If I was inclined to be interested in any other woman aside from your mother, and I wished to... er... have my way with her," My father blushed; it must be awkward talking to your almost adult daughter about sex, it certainly was the other way around!, "Then I would be within my rights to do so, so long as I had permission from her husband, or she was unmarried - without consequence. However, if these things were to happen to you, and you tried to defend yourself - harming the person attacking you - you would be the one who would be arrested. But in the Outside, there are laws against people being subjected to the wants of people's sexual habits if they do not consent. If they force the issue, they will be punished. And, if you protect yourself against them, and injure them, it is viewed as in self-defence."

"So, if you're a guy, it has got better for you? But if you have the misfortune to be born as a female, you'd be best to find a husband who will protect you as soon as possible, or you'll be harmed?"

Mama nodded, "Basically."

I frowned at her, "Then why did you come? Did you know it would be like this? Why did you come?"

She looked to my father mouthing 'sorry', to which he smirked and waved his hand for her to go ahead, "Because, on the outside, we would have had nobody. As you know, we were young, scared and pregnant. I had no family, I grew up in the foster system," She glanced at me, she had explained the foster system to me before, and it didn't seem pleasant, "Everett's parents and siblings were joining GreyBrook. They held on to ideals that were similar to those held by the founder of GreyBrook, that women were gaining too much power with the advent a movement that had a large amount of famous women coming forward to allege that famous men had done things to them that were illegal, both in the past, and the present. This made more women come forward, who weren't famous. Creating a movement."

I frowned, "What was so bad about that? If it was illegal there, then wouldn't coming forward be a good thing?"

A sad smile passed over her face, "You'd think so. But, as you can see in what happened today, it's not here in GreyBrook. And that was the problem outside. Many people felt that the rights of men were being threatened, that they were having things taken away from them by these women coming forward. Even the ruler of the largest, most powerful nation on the planet felt the same. So, a group came together, with Ellwood Marshall and a city like GreyBrook was formed, to be filled with like-minded people."

"Except..."

"Except, there were a few of us who had no choice, if we wanted to have the help of our families in raising our own," She appeared thoughtful, gazing at my father, "Perhaps we may have made other decisions if we didn't have you to think about, or perhaps we made the right one."

I threw my hands in the air, "What do you mean? You've just spent all this time telling me it's bad, and I can see it's.... not what I would like to it be, but now you say you've made the right choice? I'm more confused now than I was before!"

She smiled and pulled a piece of paper out of the pile my father had gathered up, covered in scrawls, and ideas, "Perhaps we are where we are meant to be, to effect change. To encourage that one person who might be the one to effect change. Perhaps not now, perhaps not even in my lifetime. But they will be found, I know they will."

I peered at the paper, not understand anything on it, nor what my mother was on about, including the wistful look she gave. I crumpled my face in defeat, then a thought occurred to me, and I humoured her a little.

"Like a hero, Mama?"

She smiled, a serene smile, ill-fitting for the conversation we had just been having. "Yes, that's it! A hero, one we will see ourselves in. She will not realise it straight away, but we will. We will recognise the hero for who she is."

Was that what GreyBrook needed? A hero? Or would we have to save ourselves before she got here?

CHAPTER 3

GreyBrook was eerily quiet after the punishment display. People going about their business, women making sure they were inside before curfew. It was business as usual, with a side of quiet defeat, in both women and men. I was learning to keep my head down, not be noticed, but in doing so was noticing other people around me, and the little ways in which life had changed since the punishment was broadcast.

A slow darkness was creeping into people's lives, like they were living with a shadow that followed them around. It was as though those who were not part of the group that initial day prior to the punishment were dismayed at the display of behaviour of their fellow city dwellers. Our group had not been the only one whipped into a frenzy by Ellwood's rant like speech, and both others in our group and several people in other groups had been harmed, I'd been told. No one was speaking of what happened, but of people who had been forcefully removed from their group of women and taken away, who may not have been seen again, at least in the weeks since the frenzy. Some had returned, but as only a shell of themselves, at least to those around them who knew them well.

For those caught up in the emotion of the frenzied groups, who had been called to action by Ellwood's words to pursue the unmarried women with renewed vigour, it was perhaps not as quiet as it was for everyone else. The darkness still lurked, they were difficult to pick from the others, aside from their lack of trying to keep their interest in women under wraps. It was like they felt just a tiny wee bit of guilt after the punishment. Those I noticed this most in were around my parents age, so it could have been a hangover from Before, from the Outside. I wasn't sure.

EVENTUALLY THOSE WHO had disappeared returned. Never the same as before they disappeared - thin, broken, haunted. They did not speak of the horror they must have endure, given the looks in their eyes. They knew better than to draw the wrath of Ellwood, and what accounted for law around here. Within small circles, they were known as the "Taken", never to their face, and never around those who had cheered on Ellwood's punishment - no one wanted that inflicted on another woman who hadn't even spoken out, that we had assumed was "taken". I assumed most women did not wish to be within their ranks either.

Life moved on. The effect that the display of punishment had created carried on for quite some time, becoming part of the way of life in GreyBrook, so much so that we forgot how it had been to start with - we kept quiet about treatment we found abhorrent, and we stayed safe from beatings, and public whipping. Whispers about the Taken slowed, even though women continued to disappear.

"HEY, ISA! WAIT." I was hurrying home, whilst the curfew was no longer in effect, I didn't like to waste my time getting home after work: better safe than sorry I figured given I was still unmarried, still 'available'. I dreaded being asked anything by anyone, for fear I'd have to take them up on their offer to stay within the law. I knew this voice though. It belonged to the young man I met at the billboard on that fateful day. The one who didn't understand why we had to bear witness to the cruelty.

"Hey, Cormac, how goes things?" I slowed my pace, to allow him to catch up.

"They're good. You?"

"Yeah, good. I don't see you round so much anymore, where are you now?"

"Training or working in the fields," He smiled, a smile that did funny things to my knees, weakening them somehow.

"Training for?"

"You know how they're thinking having us all in the one big city won't work long term?" I nodded, "They've decided to split us along work related lines so there is a group for produce, for security, for medical and religious needs, for technology and communication, and for teaching and education. I kind of want to help where I can without being violent, so I'm thinking I'll try out for the medical group,"

"Isn't it medical and religious?" I asked with a small grin on my face, which Cormac returned, "How will that work? You aren't of the faith of Ellwood, and his cronies."

"I know, but I figure I'll figure it out when I need to. I'm just not sure about having to follow the religious rules regarding what happens in one's home."

I frowned, this bit I hadn't heard of, "What do you mean?"

"Well, you know the book Ellwood is forever reading passages from? It denotes punishments for disobeying orders, and the 'proper' place of a woman within a relationship," He looked disgusted, then wiped the emotion off his face in case someone could see him, "I don't agree with it, but if I get into that group. Sections, I think he's thinking of calling them. If I get into that Section, I will have to treat my wife as property, should I ever get a wife. It doesn't sit right with me."

I smiled, "Surely, what happens in your own home is beyond their reach?"

"It could be, but by the time I get there, the rules might have changed."

"Well, I think you'll make someone a wonderful husband at some stage in your future, and you can work it out between you." He smiled, ducking his head embarrassed. I stopped to see what he was doing, twiddling his fingers in his belt loops, scuffing his feet. I ended up having to walk back to him to get him to keep moving with me.

"Thanks, Isa. It means a lot," he looked up through his long eyelashes, watching my face, as I stared quizzically at him.

"Come on then," I urged, "Time to get ho-"

Suddenly my mouth had been covered by his, his hands grasping the sides of my head, his kiss incredibly gentle. At first, I wanted to push him away, startled, and started to try to, but began to enjoy the kiss, kissing him back, taking hold of him until we both parted breathless. He blushed, ducking his head again

"Well... that was unexpected," I muttered, as he glanced at me, "But pleasant!" I reached for him this time, and kissed him myself, much to his surprise. This time when we parted, a grin was plastered across his face.

"Well, that went a lot better than I expected. I'm sorry I sprung that on you, but I didn't know how to tell you I really like you, and... really wanted to do... that." I smiled,

"I'm kind of glad you did," I blushed, as he scuffed his feet like a schoolboy.

Conversation got awkward after that, as he joined me on my walk home, before turning back to head to his own home. I had told no one, but I'd been thinking about him on and off since we met at the punishment display. He seemed different to the other guys around me, gentler, but strong in his own way. And, yeah, I thought he was attractive. I wandered into the house, a small smile on my face, that neither of my parent caught that day - which was a good thing, I didn't want to explain myself yet, when I had no idea what there was to explain.

WE MET UP A FEW TIMES, over the coming months, hanging out and chatting, and he even came for dinner. A grin plastered all over my mother's face was more embarrassing than the silly stories my father told. Later on, he laughed as I apologised for their behaviour.

"Oh, Isa. It's their job to embarrass you at every opportunity. It's their payment for those terrible toddler years, apparently."

I cuffed him on the arm, "How would you know? You don't have kids!"

He ducked out of my way, giggling. "Not yet, but it is the gospel according to my mother - it's her turn to get back at me. Are you saying she lied to me? It's not their job?!" He feigned shock, as I laughed at his antics, before he took my hand, becoming serious, "And, I meant, not yet. But one day. One day it'll be our job." He winked, letting go of my hand and walking away, a secret smile on his face.

TURNING, I WALKED BACK into the house to find my parents mulling over the stack of papers on the table again. They hadn't pulled them out in months.

"Okay, what is going on?"

My father put his finger to his lips and made a slight movement of his hand towards my mother. I glanced at her, frowning at him, until what I had seen on her face registered with my brain, and I looked back.

Her face relaxed, eyes unfocused, she looked as though she had taken some medication that didn't agree with her. A pen clutched in her hand, resting over a blank sheet of paper. A slight furrow of concentration on her brow was all that told me she was even in there. A twitch of her lip, just prior to her scribbling something on the paper in front of her. My father finally looked away from me, and down to what she was writing, a smile forming on his face. This continued in silence for some time, as I watched a strange dance play out in front of me, a dance it was clear Merin and Everett Scott had danced many times. Sitting down, I watched them working together, my mother unfocused, my father attentive to her every move, sliding more paper under her pen when she ran out of space.

He slid them away from me on purpose, shaking his head when I reached for them, a head tilt towards my mother, as though she needed to explain what they meant, and couldn't do that just now. I waited, curious to see what the hell was going on.

Suddenly she startled, blinking, dropping the pen which my father picked up and moved out of the way. She glanced around, her eyes in focus now, searching for something. Until they came to rest on my father's face. It was as though he was her anchor in a world of storm-swept waves. The moment she found him, the panic gone from her face, a soft smile replacing it. I was trying not to interrupt their moment, a twitch in my leg making my foot thump on the floor, startling her out of her daze. Tearing her gaze from my father, she searched out the cause of the noise.

"Sorry Mama," I murmured, hating that I'd broken the trance, as she searched my face looking for something. Apparently finding it, she smiled and yawned. Standing, silent, she nodded at my father and walked out of the room. He watched her go, then collected the papers from the table.

"She'll need a sleep after that. Don't worry, she will explain later. Much better than I ever could. I just make sure she has enough paper and collect everything after."

I wasn't sure what the hell was going on, or what any of the writing on the paper meant. I set about making something for dinner for the three of us and pondered what had just occurred as I busied myself with preparation. There was something going on that my parents had hidden from me all these years. Why had they hidden it? It was weird, yes, but it was my mother - I wouldn't judge her for it. Was she unwell? I wasn't sure what to think. Chopping potatoes to boil, I shrugged to myself, and figured that they would tell me when they were ready, but now I'd witnessed whatever it was in person, it would be soon.

"ISA, THANK YOU FOR getting dinner on," a small, tired voice murmured behind me, startling me out of my daze.

"Mama, how are you feeling?"

She gave an exhausted looking smile, "Tired, but that's normal," she sighed, "I suppose you want to know what all that was?"

"Um... only if you want to tell me?"

She smiled, taking my hand, "Everett! Finish up in here, will you?"

A sigh came from the direction my father had been, grumbling as he closed his book, thumping it down on the table, his knee clicking as he stood up from his favourite chair.

"Yes, Merrin," He beamed a smile at her as he passed us to get to the kitchen - the fuss he'd made was all just him being silly.

Sitting at the table, Mama pulled a couple of papers out of the pile on the table, pushing them towards me.

"Isabella, I know what you saw earlier was confusing. I'd like to explain, but you may be more confused by the end of the conversation, than you are now."

I glanced down at the papers, scrawls in my mother's handwriting. I could make out "Black, hero, young" on the first page, the following one had "She will wear black" and "Small, but mighty". None of it made sense to me.

"What's it all about, Ma?"

Rubbing her head, she chewed on her bottom lip before answering, "Have you ever heard of deja vu? It's kind of like that, "I frowned, but let her continue, "It has happened all my life, but until today I've only ever told your father. I get weird flashes, or visions, from time to time, usually when I'm under stress or up-set."

"Visions of?"

"Things that haven't happened yet. As a kid, it might happen later that day or the next day. But as I got older, the visions are more involved and can be quite some time away."

I waved the papers at her, "These are visions?"

"Yes. I don't always know what they mean, or when they will come to pass. But they ALWAYS come the same way, and they ALWAYS happen. I tried to deny it, but... that just made them worse."

"And these are coming soon?"

She tilted her head at me, eyes wild with bewilderment, "So you believe me? You don't think I'm mad?"

I shrugged, "Ma, I don't know what to believe at the moment, but I know what I saw, and what you're telling me might explain that, so I believe you at the moment."

"Thank you. You have no idea how much it means you trust me on this. Even in the outside, people like me are looked at funny, if not put away for being 'off in the head' so I never mentioned it, until your father caught me in the middle of one before we came to GreyBrook."

I looked up, "Did you get any visions about coming here?"

She blushed and lowered her head, "I did."

"And?"

"They came true," I frowned, until she continued, "They're not always bad, or scary things. The positive ones come true too. It was both before we came in, and yes, both sides have come to pass." I looked down at the papers again, remembering the pile on the table.

"These ones?"

She smiled, "I've been getting a lot in the last few months, ever since the punishment for those two women was broadcast. Most of it seems positive, but it appears it will be a LONG time before they come to pass. All I know is that there will be a hero for GreyBrook - one who will stand up, and force change that GreyBrook needs. Change it needs now but won't get. One vision made it appear the hero we need isn't born yet, and sadly won't realise she's the hero GreyBrook needs on her own."

I reached for the other papers, "So, what are we doing with this then?" There was sheet after sheet of paper with pictures, and scrawls on it.

My father poked his head around the corner as I asked, "We're thinking of putting it into a book, putting it in places that people can find it, and... do with it what they will. Anonymously." He added,

"Good idea," I took a long hard look at both of them. They were both invested in this, in each other. My father believed with everything he had in my mother's ability. You could see it in the way he looked at her, nothing but commitment and love in his eyes. A similar look graced her face, but with a difference. She looked as though she felt completely safe with him, that he would never give her secret away, and never doubt her. I smiled, hoping that one day I found someone to look at in the same way.

"I'm in."

CHAPTER 4

Mama continued to 'receive' visions building on the ones she'd already had. Work began in earnest, compiling everything she had 'seen' into a book. Papa was planning on printing a few at a time, at the end of a shift at his work, building slowly enough he wouldn't get caught until we had enough.

GREYBROOK AND ITS BEGINNINGS were slowly being replaced. Anything we knew of Before, or the Outside, was being replaced by what we could only call propaganda from Ellwood, or at least to those who knew of the true history of GreyBrook. That was his plan, that people would eventually forget just how GreyBrook came to be, or the reasons why, and perhaps even be convinced that there was nothing outside of GreyBrook, erasing the history of a huge number of original GreyBrook residents. Writing the changes into law, with a clause added to make it almost impossible to change in the future, whether Ellwood was in charge or not. What had scared them so much that they needed to erase where they came from so drastically? Would it not have been better for them to focus on the parts of Before, and the Outside that had caused the creation of the City, to prove it's worth?

"WE CANNOT FORGET WHERE we came from!" My mother was shouting at my father.

"Honey, I know! Keep your voice down!" he hissed, waving at me as I stepped into the room to shut the windows. If she wouldn't stop shouting, the neighbours would report her and us for treason.

"Those who forget the past are destined to repeat it," she muttered, glaring at my father, "he can't do this to GreyBrook. He can't do this to us." An exasperated sigh gave away just how frustrated she was with the situation. I frowned, trying to figure out how to fix it, in a way that wouldn't get us in trouble.

"Why not add the history of Before, and the Outside to the book?" I muttered, 'The entire book is illegal, so why not go out with a bang?" I grinned, as Mama blinked at me, a sort of joyous shock on her face.

"Oh, you wonderful child! That's perfect!" She grabbed my face, stood on her toes and kissed my forehead before flitting off to get started. My father winked at me as he shook his head. Laughing, I realised she was lucky he loved her without condition, she was making him grey with all of this lately.

"Papa, I'm heading off to meet Meredith, and will probably stay at Cormac's tonight." He nodded, waving me off.

AS AN UNMARRIED, BUT eligible and of age woman, we'd all decided it was safest for me to continue to live at home until I was married. It wasn't all that unusual for girls of my age to be doing the same, or married, even though as an adult it felt a little weird having to tell my parents I would be staying with my boyfriend. But I understood their reasoning and felt just that little bit safer knowing someone would worry if I was missing.

I walked to where Meredith and I had agreed to meet. Waiting in the street, in the open, felt a little exposed even though it wasn't dark yet. As it got darker, I couldn't make much out in the distance, feeling a little insecure at the fact I couldn't see trouble coming until it was too late. Meredith was never late, I was starting to worry, but couldn't stay much longer. Curfew wasn't all that far away, and I didn't relish the thought of being put in the cells for breaking it. I waited until the last minute for her, before heading to Cormac's, all the time worrying about where she'd gotten to.

Cormac could see I was worried about Meredith, but with no way to contact her all that worrying was just ruining my evening with him. Ellwood had finally removed all forms of communication via telephone - landline, and cellular. The only people who could communicate without seeing each other were those in his security team. It made life decidedly awkward to organise. Cormac kept trying to take my mind off Meredith, distracting me with random bits of news.

"Did you see that Ellwood has decided that we aren't productive enough as we are," I frowned at him, but let him continue, "He's talking about separating us further."

"How?" I wasn't sure where either of them, Ellwood or Cormac, was going with this.

"By groups of useful professions apparently. One each for produce, health or healing, education, security, and communications." I nodded, still distracted, cutting the onions for whatever Cormac was cooking for dinner. He could tell I wasn't listening, "Love, set the table for dinner, I'll bring it through soon."

IT WAS A BEAUTIFUL meal, the different flavours creating such an interesting combination of tastes in my mouth, I was distracted from worrying about Meredith, and a lot of other things, including having a conversation. I could see Cormac smiling as I devoured the meal, but it wasn't until he pulled his chair close to mine, I realised he wanted to talk to me.

"Isa, I know we are young, and perhaps not yet ready, " Startled, I dropped my fork onto the plate in front of me and turned to face him, "But, I'm certain we are destined to be together. I feel like I would be incomplete without you, and that nothing would fill that void." He paused to smiled, reaching into his pocket, "Isabella Maria Scott, will you marry me?"

I gaped at him, completely taken by surprise by his request and the simple band he held in front of me, "Yes, Cormac, I will."

The smile on his face as he slipped the simple gold band over my finger told me he had had this planned for some time, particularly when he looked up and found me frowning slightly.

"Isa, it's okay. I asked your father a few weeks ago, and he was more than happy to give his blessing." I grinned, that explained some weird behaviour on my father's behalf. It was also law that a woman's father must give permission – something about the way of the faith that had begun GreyBrook. If those who were wed, much like my parents would have been had my mother's family joined her here, without their families blessing were dealt with severely.

He took my face in his hands, and kissed me, only pulling away when we both needed to breathe.

"I love you, Cormac Joe Masters."

"And I you, Isabella Maria Scott," He got a cheeky look on his face as he said my name, squeezing my hand.

"Oi, I've just eaten. I'm not... ready for that yet!"

He scrunched up his face in confusion, then laughed, "Oh, I wasn't asking you to race to the bedroom... though, I wouldn't say no! I was thinking, I like Scott for a last name, and you have no brothers to continue the family name. I would like to become Mr Scott, rather than you Mrs Masters." I gazed at him, pondering what that would mean for us legally. It wasn't illegal, just frowned upon because it gave the woman the power in part of a relationship, when it was believed that she should obey her husband. But from memory, in situations like ours, where I was the last of our Scott line, we could do it.

"I would love that, Mr soon-to-be Scot," and kissed him back.

MAMA HAD NOT KNOWN of Cormac's request for my hand, until the following day when we made the announcement. It wasn't until she saw the knowing grin on Papa's face, she put two and two together and remembered the law.

"You didn't tell me!"

He shook his head, "It was their surprise, love."

"Oh, and what a wonderful surprise it is," I wondered why she hadn't had a vision, but then I figured she got usually had visions of warning now, and well, what was there to warn about a happy situation?

"Oh, and Mr Scott, I'd like to take your surname if I may. To continue the line of Scott, instead of it ending with Isabella," Papa frowned, trying to remember what the rules around it were.

"Do you have brothers, Cormac?" Ah, that was the sticking point, if he didn't, and my father wouldn't know, he couldn't take my surname. I smiled, as Cormac answered as I knew he would.

"Yes, sir. Simon is already married, and his wife has taken the Masters name, as she has a brother."

Papa grinned and extended his hand. "Then yes, you may. Welcome to the family, Mr Scott."

Cormac snorted, "Cormac, sir. Mr Scott is my father-in-law." As Papa cuffed him on the shoulder, laughing.

AMID ALL THE CELEBRATION, there was a knock at the door. Answering it, I found Ewan Marshall, Meredith's father, standing outside, looking concerned.

"Excuse my intrusion in your day, Isabella, but have you seen Meredith since you met up last night?" I gasped,

"Mr Marshall, she never turned up last night. I couldn't contact you to ask if she had stayed home, but I had to assume she had. Did she not?" I could hear my family coming up behind me.

"No, she didn't. She left to meet you, and that was the last we saw of her."

"Her security detail?"

"He saw her to the train, but left her there as is what he usually does when she comes to visit with you," He sighed, "She sticks out with a security detail if she comes here, where there is none, so she refuses to have them with her." I hadn't realised this, having assumed that he was there, in the shadows, keeping an eye on her from a far, to give us some privacy.

"I'm sorry Mr Marshall, but I haven't seen her. I'm worried about her now though, I thought she had just stayed home!"

I heard my father step up behind me, "Ewan, if we see her, I will personally make sure she gets home to you. Please let us know anything we can do to help find her." He announced,

"Thank you, Everett. I'm hoping it's all a big misunderstanding, and she went to a different friend's place yesterday, and will be home when I get there,"

"I hope so too, but I'm going out to see if I can find her. Aren't we, Cormac?" He nodded.

"Thank you, Isabella. I will go now and see what our search party has uncovered. Please keep me up to date." He bid us farewell. I turned to my parents as I shut the door behind him.

"I meant what I said, I'm just getting more comfortable shoes,"

Mama nodded, "we know, love. We will look for her too, cover more ground."

DESPITE A THOROUGH search of a large area of GreyBrook by foot that day, and many times over the next few weeks, there was no sign of Meredith. Leader Ellwood broadcast about her going missing several times over the loudspeaker and billboards, flashing her face over the billboards several times a day for most of the month. Given her position within the Marshall family, they were making a huge fuss, one I'd like to think would have been given to all those who had gone missing, but I knew in my heart hadn't been. So many people from my area had going missing and turned up a week later very different - never any fuss aside from the concern of their family and friends.

I'd overheard grumblings of others I worked with, that no such fuss would have been made had it have been them, or for a few when it was them.

"It's just because she's part of the Elite. How is she any better than us? Bet you she would look down her nose at us and not give two shits if we were missing." I heard muttered in my vicinity one day.

"Hey, she's a friend of mine," I blurted out, before I thought through what I was doing, "And, no she wouldn't, she doesn't. She hates being in the Confederate Circle. Says it feels fake and superficial. I know for a fact she worried about the girls from here when they went missing." They looked just mildly ashamed.

"But... none of us would ever get this much publicity. Those women punished via the billboards a while back, the only publicity they got was when they blamed someone, instead of themselves."

I nodded, "I know. The power of who you know I suppose. I understand the frustration, but right now, I just want to find her and make sure she's okay."

They nodded and left me alone.

PUBLICITY DIED DOWN after a while, and Meredith was still missing. Cormac and I planned a small gathering of family and friends to marry us. I thought of her often whilst planning, we'd talked about it before we had boyfriends, what we could do if we ever got married. I'd never wanted anything big; family and a few friends would do me. With Meredith missing, this was all I wanted. Cormac's brother had experienced a large wedding, and he didn't want the fuss of one as large, so was more than happy with a small gathering of our closest family and friends. The atmosphere was lovely, though missing the laughter that Meredith would have brought to it, but the company was great, and the food delicious. It went off without a hitch. Suddenly, I was moving out of home, and into Cormac's smaller place. An adult, decisions that had once been that of my parents was now mine, or Cormac's to make. Weirdly liberating, and scary at the same time.

SEVERAL MONTHS INTO the marriage, we found out I was pregnant. Everyone was excited about the possibility of new life, except for one thing.

"I'm looking forward to meeting this new bundle of wonder, love," Mama started, her face twisting as though she had something else, something not completely complimentary to say, "I have to say one thing though." There it was.

"What's that, Mama?" My hands protectively covering my barely existent bulge unconsciously as I sat at the table with her. A position my hands found themselves in a lot, but I'd noticed that many others pregnant women stood or sat the same way, so I no longer thought it was weird.

She shifted uncomfortably, "Please don't hate me for saying this, love. But I hope it's not a little girl. I hope it's a little boy, and he will grow up like your father and your husband - gentle and caring, unwilling to harm another. But a girl... in this city? With the way it's going?"

I smiled, I understood what she meant. I had my own concerns about this baby being a female, but also another theory.

"What if she was the hero your visions speak of? The hero that GreyBrook needs?"

Mama looked up, a sparkle in her eyes, an edge of sadness. "That would be amazi-" She cut off, as though she had been interrupted, but by a thought, "Sorry, it would be amazing, but whilst you have something to do with the hero, it's not the baby in your belly. They will be amazing too, but not the hero."

I couldn't help but be both intrigued by the comment she had made about my involvement, and sad that it wouldn't be the baby in my belly.

THE BOOK WAS FINISHED, being printed slowly by my father until we felt we had enough to distribute. Once it was out there, it would be difficult to print more, so we needed to have as many copies as we could give out ready to go before we started. Mother had tried to figure out exactly what would happen, what the actions of the hero would culminate in, but despite trying her hardest, she could never see it. In the end, she just smiled

"It's up to her. I can't see it, because in the end, it's up to her what will happen. It's in her hands, and only her hands. Not the Gods, not the spirits, not whoever it is giving me these visions. Hers, and hers alone. And, that's okay." And closed the book, smiling, "It's done. It's up to her now."

CHAPTER 5

The little black book, or the Book of Prophecies as my parents were calling it - and had printed on its little cover, was all Mama had hoped for. It was as though her dreams of doing something with the 'skill' she had been endowed with from childhood had finally come true, and Mama seemed much more relaxed than I had ever seen her, despite it being more dangerous than ever to have the information we had, in the form we had it.

We were standing around the table, Cormac at work, trying to figure out how to get these books out in the public without anyone knowing it was us, or breaking curfew, when there was a knock at the door. Mama startled, sweeping the books into a box, rushing upstairs with the small amount we had had on the table, before she allowed Papa to open the door.

"Morning, Ewan," Papa had been having more contact with the Marshall family, particularly Ewan since Meredith's disappearance, but also with Ellwood. He figured it might keep the book thing under the radar.

"Everett, I come with news," Ewan announced, walking through the door. I moved into the kitchen, to hear the news. Ewan looked down, eyes widening at the bump on my front, "I see you also have some!" Papa glanced at me, smiling.

"You come with news of Meredith?" Papa asked him, the polite thing to do was let Ewan finish his announcement before acknowledging the news in our home.

"I do," My own eyes wide, I made full eye contact with Ewan, something not usually tolerated by the Marshall men and those higher in GreyBrook, but this time he let it happen, "She has returned."

There were gasps all around the room, as I stammered, "Is... Is... Is she okay?"

There was a pause before he replied,

"I think so," a slight tremor in his voice, "She wants to see you, Isabella, if okay with your..." He took a purposeful glance at my stomach, his eyes grazing my hands as he swept them up again, smiling, "Husband."

I grinned, "He is at work, but I will get a message to him, to gain permission to come to see Meredith," He nodded, "Would it be okay to accompany you? Could you wait momentarily whilst I gain permission from Cormac?" I could feel my mother tensing behind me at my use of the formal language towards Ewan, when it wasn't how I had been raised - I was the boss of my own body, and I didn't have to do anything I wasn't comfortable doing.

"I am happy with that. Where does your husband work?"

"He's an emergency tech just down the road. We could walk past on the way to the train?" He nodded. I turned to Mama and winked, watching her relax as she figured out I just wanted to be on his good side to get to Meredith, that I hadn't jumped the fence to go completely GreyBrook. I would need all the practice I could get though, if the proposed Sections were coming into play soon.

I walked into the place that Cormac worked, the receptionist summoning him to come to the front desk. He frowned as he walked through and noticed Ewan Marshall waiting outside.

"What's going on, love?"

"I'm pretending to ask you for permission to accompany him to see Meredith."

His eyes widened at her name, as I smiled. Smiling back, he nodded whilst murmuring, "I'm glad you said pretending, I'd hate to think you thought you had to ask. Go, see her. I will see you when you get home." I hugged him and left.

THE TRIP WAS AWKWARD. Neither Ewan nor I knew how to talk casually with the other, so we spent the trip sitting silently, trying to avoid eye contact. As we neared the Confederate Circle, Ewan cleared his throat, startling me. I glanced over, concerned.

"Isabella, I just wanted to warn you. Meredith.... She's...." He frowned, trying to find the right words, "She's different. Damaged." His face screwed up in disgust at himself for referring to his own daughter in such a way.

Swallowing, I nodded, "Thank you for warning me, Mr Marshall."

MEREDITH WAS SITTING in her room, back to the door, staring out the window. I paused in the doorway, watching the way the light framed her silhouette, her darkened form still the way I could remember her from last time I had seen her, wanting to remember her that way as long as I could.

"Isa?" She turned as I took more steps into her room, "Isa, is that you?"

"It is, Mere," There was a small squeal of excitement, a grunt of pain as she pushed herself out of her chair, making her way towards me, a smile gracing a bruised, and scarred face. Fighting to keep the shock from my face, I opened my arms to her.

"Not too tight," a whisper escaped as she embraced me. I kept my arms light over her shoulders, fighting not to squeeze her tight, scared of hurting her. When she finally pulled away, she looked down, her eyes lighting upon the slight bump I had under my shirt. I rubbed a hand over it, watching her face, as she looked back at me, questions running all over it. I had used my left hand out of habit, and she'd also glimpsed the plain band Cormac had given me as a wedding band.

"We tried to wait, love," my voice cracked, "I so badly wanted you there." She glanced at me, a quirk to her lip, as she reached out to touch my belly, as I nodded my consent to the touch.

"It's okay, Isa. I was gone a long time," She continued to stroke my belly as she murmured, "How far along?"

"About halfway now I think." She smiled again, pulling my hand to make me sit down on the bench seat by the window. The light from outside now illuminated just how badly she had been injured and disfigured. My beautiful friends face was covered in thin white scars, marring her youthful face, bruising over her cheek bones, and around her neck fading into that awful yellow colour around the edges. Her eyes still held a cheeky sparkle, but it seemed dulled today, pain surfacing from time to time that wasn't physical.

"Promise me, if it's a girl, you'll call her Rachel." There was a pleading in her eyes.

"I'd have to get Cormac on board, but if I can, we can if it's a girl. What's the big thing with the name?" My hand slipped from my belly to take her hand,

"It's my middle name. Or... one of them."

"You've got more than one?!"

She chuckled, "Yeah, apparently several Aunties that wanted in on it, when I was born."

"What are the others? I'm boring, I've only got Maria."

"I'm apparently, officially, Meredith Rebekah Melissa Rachel Marshall"

I nodded, impressed. "That seems like a lot of writing on official forms!"

She chuckled again, a sad note to the edge of the sound as though she felt wrongdoing so, and that it hurt her to laugh. "It is! Rachel was my favourite one though. Don't tell the others!"

My turn to chuckle, "I won't," I watched her face for a few moments, squeezing her hand, "Meredith, are you okay?"

Her eyes filled with tears, as she pulled her hand from mine to wipe them away, a choked sound as she lost the battle, and let them spill down her face.

"No." She squeaked, wiping at her face, reaching for me. We hugged as she sobbed, until she pulled away, wiping her face. "But I will be."

"You know you ca-"

"No, I can't." She narrowed her eyes at me, as I finally caught on.

"Oh... Jesus," I muttered, squeezing her hand, "Yes, you can. I'd never tell anyone. Just know that. If you ever need to, I'm here." She nodded, glancing at the door. Pausing, I heard footsteps in the hallway, solid and sure, much like her father's. I nodded to her I understood, just before his head came around the corner.

"Isabella, I trust you will require an escort to return home this evening?" His voice made it obvious that I could not stay the night, and I knew better than to push my luck. I could see that Meredith would have preferred it, but she didn't have the energy to fight back against her father.

"That I will, Mr Marshall. Thank you."

"I shall organise one of Meredith's detail to escort you home." He nodded and left again.

Meredith looked broken, as I turned back to her.

"I don't want you to go," She whispered, "I'm stuck here with two people who tiptoe around me like I'll break, but who won't allow me to speak of what happened. Who would report me to Uncle Ellwood in a heartbeat."

Shocked, I stared at her, "Your own family would report you to Ellwood?"

"They're sticklers for the rules," She paused, sighing, "I get it. They have to be a good example. Can't have the Grand Leader's family breaking the rules, and getting away with it, can you?"

I shook my head sadly, "I guess not," Taking her hands in mine, "When you can, come and stay with Cormac and I. Cormac will vouch for you if your father has issues with it. The man knows better than to argue with me."

She chuckled, "You found a good one then?"

I nodded, "He's wonderful, and I can't wait for you to meet him. He... gets me."

"I'm glad, and I can't wait to meet him," She took my hand, forcing me to look her in the eyes, "Thank you for coming today, it meant a lot to me."

"I missed you, Mere. I'm so happy you're back. Just remember, I'm always here." The security escort and Ewan Marshall were at the door, waiting for me. I hugged her once more and left.

THE SECURITY DETAIL accompanied me to the door of my home with Cormac, barely saying a word as we travelled, leaving me plenty of time to think, which was the best thing he could have done.

Meredith, by saying very little, had told me all I needed to know. I was bubbling with a mixture of anger, sadness and pain. I didn't think I would be capable of holding back should he encourage me into conversation, so I was glad he was the silent type. She had been harmed in so many ways, and her family were continuing to allow that harm to hurt her by not allowing her to talk about it, based on rules that punished those who were harmed by others, rather than those who did the harming. I had seen by the look on her face, that she needed to talk about it, needed someone else to know what had happened, so she wasn't suffering alone.

It didn't seem fair she would have to hold her pain inside, never speak of it to anyone else, but that those who had caused her such pain could discuss just what they had done with their friends, laughing and joking about abhorrent acts. Acts that would have seen them punished on the Outside, given what Mama had told me, but in GreyBrook were not seen as abhorrent, but as a rite of passage for many of the folk around me. That they could cause someone so much pain over such a long time made me suspicious of all those around me aside from my family and Cormac.

To speak of what bubbled under the surface could see both Meredith and I thrown in prison, beaten like those two women when we were younger, and several since then. Not to mention, Meredith hadn't actually said anything out loud.

I THANKED THE SECURITY detail as he made his handover of me to Cormac. A curt nod and he was gone, Cormac waiting until he was out of sight before closing the door.

"How was she?" He asked, his eyes fixed on my face, brow furrowed in concern.

I pondered my words for a moment, "She's broken, but she will fight through," was all I could manage.

"What happened?"

"She was Taken, Cormac." He gasped, hand flying to his mouth.

"She told you that?" That was what he was shocked about?

I shook my head, "No, she didn't need to. I could see it by the scars on her face, the bruising healing on her neck and cheekbones, the dark sadness in her eyes, her admission she could not speak of it - even to her parents." Anger was causing me to splutter.

"Sorry," He murmured, "It's just it's so illegal to talk about it, I was surprised she had told you. But... she didn't. Not really. Did she?"

"No, but she got the point across without using the words," I was pacing, as he watched me leaning against the kitchen bench, "I'm just so damn angry about the whole thing. How dare someone think they have a right to do such a thing?"

Cormac just stared at me, he knew my feelings on GreyBrook, but this was a different look, a bewildered one. "Isa, it's GreyBrook - you know why they think they have a right. It's because they DO have that right. Remember?" I spun around, glaring at him, as he continued, "in fact, if I wanted to, I could go out and have any woman I wished, whether she wished it or not. Because that is how GreyBrook works. You know I don't believe it's right, but you seem to think GreyBrook has changed, and will change - it won't. This will always be seen as Meredith's own fault - why was she not with her security detail, with the luck she has to even have one - you don't. Why was she out there? What was she wearing? Who's to say she didn't want it to happen?"

I had stormed up to him, panting, glaring at him almost toe-to-toe. "How dare you say those things, Cormac!" I hissed, not wanting to alert the neighbours to what seemed like our first fight, "What if this baby is a girl? Would you still say those things?"

Cormac shook his head sadly, "Isabella, you aren't listening. I believe none of those things. But I am but one man, and GreyBrook is not me, I am not GreyBrook. GreyBrook and many of the men in it will view her like that should they ever find out, even other women. You seem to expect it to be different, but it's GreyBrook - GreyBrook will always resist change like the Plague! Remember why it was built in the first place? Why it was REALLY built." I took a few steps back, looking up at him, shoulder slumped in defeat.

"Cor, I'm sorry. I... it's..." I threw my hands in the air and wandered off.

"Isa, I know. But let's do what your Mama is suggesting and see if we can change anything." He called after me.

Damn I was lucky with this one.

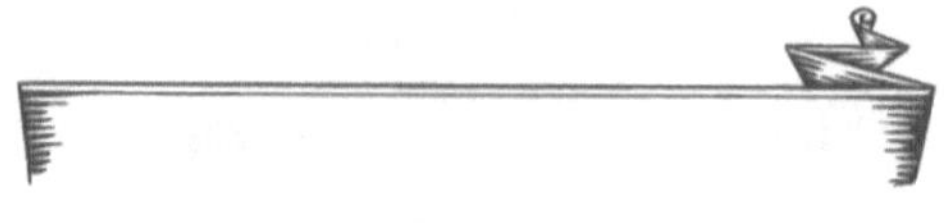

CHAPTER 6

Days later, Meredith still recovering at home, we followed through on helping Mama get her visions out there, hidden under their noses. We had had the idea of secreting some books in places like-minded people could find them, and others in places that anyone could find if they looked hard enough. Waterproofed and anonymous, we could leave them in places it was okay if they weren't found quickly.

A lot of this had to be done at dusk so we weren't seen clearly, in case someone spied us leaving the book - ideas of a time and a culture that was not Grey-Brook. It was kind of exciting to be sneaking around in the dark with Cormac at my side, leaving little books of hope all over town.

Until we got caught.

"NO, SHE DID NOT HAVE anything to do with this," I frowned at Mama, who gave me a withering look, glancing pointedly at my growing belly, "She had no idea."

"Merrin Agatha Scott, do you take full responsibility for this crime?"

"I do. Neither Everett nor Isabella had any part in this."

"And the printing of this.... filth? Does your husband not work in an industry that provides printing services?" My mother set her jaw and refused to speak, even when they tugged on the handcuffs that held her hands uncomfortably behind her back.

"Hey, don't hurt her. She's done nothing to you," She shot me a glare, trying to warn me to stay out of it.

"Merrin Agatha Scott. You are under arrest for the crime of promotion of ideas that are of the Outside and will be transported to the nearest cells to await sentencing for your crimes. Do you have anything to say for yourself?" I could see by the narrowing of her eyes, she was going to say something she'd never admit to regretting, but it would make life worse.

"It will come to pass that those who ignore the signs of the future, of the changes, will suffer the greatest. She will ensure that the suffering will last ten times as long as that which you inflicted on those you saw as lesser. Be warned." The two arresting officers looked at one another, frowning.

"Shit, can we add another charge?" One smirked as the other pondered, "Yep."

"Merrin Agatha Scott, you are also charged with spreading propaganda of the supernatural kind - forbidden within these faith-filled walls. If you continue to speak in such a way, you will be locked up in the local psychiatric facility, without trial, for the rest of your days."

"But that's no-"

"Isabella," She interrupted, "I will be okay. Please tell your father what has happened." The two officers led her away from me.

I had been going to complain that it was unjust to be held in psychiatric care without trial, when she had interrupted. I pondered why, as I watched her leave, a smile forming slowly on my lips. My view was not that which a Grey-Brook citizen typically held - the rules were the rules, and they were never questioned. I questioned everything, and she knew that. I would have caused both of us more trouble if she hadn't stopped my verbal thought in its tracks.

PAPA TRIED TO HELP her get out of the cells, pleading her case. She would have hated that he had to make her sound a little mad, a little slow, when she was in fact the complete opposite. Hated it but understood that he was only doing what the culture of GreyBrook was forcing him to do.

It didn't work.

Not that she helped herself out of the situation. She became fixated on quoting visions she had had, coming across as both threatening with her warnings, and completely crazy with her insistence they were predictions. In some small way, they succeeded together to get her moved to more comfortable, but much more permanent accommodations in the local psychiatric hospital. Once in BrookHaven Mental Hospital, you never usually left, particularly if you were there as the apparently 'criminally insane'.

She seemed more caught up in her visions, the prophecies she felt were to come, as though they were consuming her. She saw and spoke of nothing else. She was completely unaware that her arrest with the Book of Prophecies copies she had on her had pushed Ellwood Marshall to ban the colour black from books, aside from the ink, in GreyBrook. She had just smiled cheekily when she was told, a little surprised that it had prompted such a reaction.

"Could always print them in another colour?" She had suggested, trying to suppress a giggle, "He must be awful frightened by the predictions in the Book to do something that drastic. Good."

A smile twitched at the corners of my lips, "Maybe he is, Mama."

However, her seemingly lucid periods got shorter and fewer. I tried to visit as often as I was able before the end of the pregnancy. Papa visited so often that at one point he was also arrested, after being caught talking to her about the books and visions, during a rare lucid period. However, because they were happy to blame everything related to the books on my mother, as she was the easier target in GreyBrook, Papa's stay in the cells was only for a few days to 'teach him a lesson.'

RACHEL MERRIN SCOTT arrived in an awful hurry a few weeks before what would have been full term. A full head of dark hair, a good set of lungs judging by her hearty cry on arrival, and a healthy size, she was perfect in every way. Both Cormac and Papa were besotted on first meeting the little bundle of perfection, who promptly sighed in that cutesy way that only babies can at the constant doting over her.

"She's perfect, love, you've done a wonderful job," My father whispered, kissing my forehead, "Your mother will be elated to hear she is here. May I tell her the good news?" I'd nodded and laughed as he'd almost skipped out of the maternity area of the hospital, on his way to BrookHaven, which was not on site.

SETTLING INTO FAMILY life, I didn't have as much time to visit Mama in BrookHaven. Cormac was concerned about the safety of Rachel, if she was to come with me to visit the 'crazies'.

"She is visiting her Grandmother, Cormac. Your mother has met her, mine is entitled to," I'd insisted "Just because she's in BrookHaven doesn't mean she's not entitled to love on her granddaughter."

"I know, Isa. It's just... what about the others? I'm not sure your mother is as mad as they think she is, but the others... they are!" I frowned, having gotten to know a few of them whilst visiting Mama.

"Surely their families think the same thing about Mama, Cor. I'll leave if it becomes unsafe, but she's my mother. I need to take Rachel to her." There had been a knock at the door, as we had been arguing. Cormac raised his hand to stop me from continuing and answered the door.

"Meredith! Come in!" I grinned down at Rachel as I waited for Meredith to come into the lounge.

"Hey Mama!" She exclaimed, as she spied the two of us, "and who would this bundle of perfection be?"

"Meredith, meet Rachel Merrin Scott." I handed Rachel to a stunned Meredith as she sat down next to me.

"Rachel? You did it, for me?" I nodded, watching her eyes fill with happy tears, "Thank you."

"You're welcome. I liked the name - and it went well with Merrin for my mother, so Rachel it was!"

Meredith fussed over Rachel for some time, at her happiest when Rachel drifted off to sleep in her arms, spending a lot of time just watching Rachel's sleeping face.

"Oh, and Cormac," she called quietly, as he came into the lounge, "I can solve your safety problem at BrookHaven."

"How?"

"I'll go with her. I'll make sure they leave early if it gets dangerous, or rowdy." Cormac pondered for a moment and nodded.

LATER ON THAT WEEK, Meredith, Rachel and I visited Mama in BrookHaven, hoping against hope she was having a lucid day.

"Isabella Maria Scott, you had better have brought my grand-baby to see me, or you need to turn around and get her," She shouted as she glimpsed us entering the unit,

"She's here, Mama." The smile on her face warmed my heart, as she hadn't smiled much since she'd been in here.

"Let me see her then!" She reached out for the wrapped wee bundle I had in my arms, then realising she should sit down before she took hold of Rachel, she went back to an armchair and tried again. I handed Rachel over and watched her face. Her eyes welled up as she looked down at her new granddaughter.

"Merrin Scott, meet Rachel Merrin Scott,"

She looked up, letting the tears of happiness spill over her cheeks, "Rachel Merrin Scott, I'm your Nanny Merrin." To her credit, Rachel gave her the most beautiful 'gas-smile' she could muster, before announcing to the world exactly what had caused the smile, a large eruption of wind from the lower region of her little body. The shock on her grandmother's face was hilarious, as she beamed her yet another smile. She whispered, giggled and tickled Rachel, for most of the time we were there.

"Mama, I need to get Rachel home, but we'll come back in a few days, I promise." She was sad, but let us leave, hugging me on the way out.

WE VISITED REGULARLY, Rachel, Meredith and I, watching her slowly decline into madness. Perhaps it wasn't madness, perhaps she was just falling more and more into her world of fantasy, of prophecies and a more positive out-look than what was happening in GreyBrook now.

"Isa, I worry for Rachel," She uttered, one day when she wasn't particularly lucid.

"Why, Mama?" I wasn't sure if she was with us or talking to herself.

"The theory behind GreyBrook was a good idea, but Ellwood has taken it too far. What's this Sections business he's come up with? It's separating us further from each other - the best way to keep us from figuring out his plan," she looked around suspiciously, before continuing, "And keep us separate from each other, then they can get away with me. I told you it would happen, and no one believed me."

"I don't understand, Mama. The sections are designed so that the jobs that are needed to run a city in the way GreyBrook needs to be run are catered for appropriately."

She shook her head, "The security people are where?"

"All over. They've got their own section, but like the other sections, they will provide security for all sections."

"So, they aren't there, when those who wish to harm others do so. That laws will pass to the detriment of most of the citizens without anyone aware of their passing. The circle will have leaders for each section?" I nodded, "Chosen by?"

"Ellwood," I jiggled Rachel on my lap, "Ellwood Marshall."

"So, people who will do his bidding, without question. The position is to be passed down through the male line of the family, yes?"

"Yes,"

She shook her head, "If only the hero was to come in my lifetime, she could stop this. She would make it all right." She drifted off into her visions again, only glancing my way as I made to leave with Rachel.

"See you next time, Mama."

"No love," she stood, coming to hug me and peer at Rachel again, smiling, "You won't. I love you and am very proud of the women you have become, and the wee woman you will raise."

"Mama?"

"Oh, it's okay love. But, if something happens, don't believe a word these people at Brook-Haven say. Keep believing in the prophecies." She blew a kiss and waved us away.

WE COULDN'T VISIT FOR the rest of the week, child health visits for Rachel, and other life jobs got in the way. I was preparing for the two of us to visit, when there was a knock on the door.

Papa stood on my doorstep, pale, shaken. Eyes red rimmed, and bloodshot, he looked as though he'd been crying. He lifted his hands up, shaking, placing one on my shoulder, and directing me back inside.

"Isa," His voice trembled, "Is Cormac here yet?"

I frowned, "No, he's at work, why would he be home?"

"I contacted him, to come home. I... you... need him here." The door opened suddenly as he spoke, Cormac bursting through, nodding at my father.

"Everett, you called me home?" Papa nodded, directed us both to sit down.

"Cormac, thank you for coming home so quickly," He swallowed as he sat down heavily on the single seat across from us, a quick sad smile at Rachel cooing in her bouncer, "Isa, Cormac... I have some... terrible news."

My heart leapt into my mouth, as I choked out "What's happened to Mama, Papa?"

He stared at me, his mouth working as though he was chewing on the words.

"Everett?"

Papa shook his head, "Isabella, your mother was found dead this morning, in her room." My hand flew to my mouth, as he confirmed what I had quietly suspected he would say, "They say she took her own life."

I stared at him, her last words echoing in my mind, as I murmured them out loud, "Don't believe anything they say."

"What was that, Isa?" Cormac ventured,

"Her last words to me, last time we visited, were 'don't believe anything they say' if anything happened to her," A sob caught in my father's throat, a broken man sitting in front of me, "I just thought she'd drifted back into her... world. Maybe she was with us all along?"

"Isabella," My father's voice broke, as he tried to continue, "She... we... had talked about what was going on for her. She has always said that this was a possibility." He allowed a small smile of memory cross his face, "She would not let the bastards win."

A smile crossed mine as well, "Did she leave a note, Papa? She would never leave without a note."

"They wouldn't let me into her room, so I'm not sure yet. But. I agree. She would not leave without a note."

Cormac had been silent, his hand rubbing my back, "Love, right now, does it matter? We need to organise so much stuff, and they'll give you her stuff when they're done. We can find out then." I frowned at him, despite what Papa had said Mama would never kill herself, particularly not warning me like she had, and not after the birth of her first grandchild. How could he just brush it aside like that, a 'wait and see what they tell us' approach? When it was them who would be hiding things. I opened my mouth to tell him exactly what I thought, when my father interrupted.

"They have taken her body for an autopsy, as it was an unexpected death in residential care. Perhaps we will know more after that." I nodded; I didn't want to upset Papa further.

WE REMAINED IN THE house, trying to come to terms with what had happened. Waiting for news from the coroner, and autopsy. Papa didn't want to be alone, so fussed over Rachel whilst Cormac set about organising the necessaries for a funeral in GreyBrook. A few days passed in a daze, running on autopilot, memories of my Mama surfacing when I least expected them, or when Rachel did something I would have told her about. Cormac found me kneeling on the floor sobbing more than once and gently held me until I could get my wits about me again. Meredith visited, helping with the organisation of the funeral, and collecting her items from her room.

"Father knows the coroner, I can get him to talk to him, and see if there is anything that didn't match up. I'm with you, Isa, I can't see your Mama doing that. I'll see if there is anything I can find out, but first we need to get her stuff from BrookHaven. Your dad isn't up to it, but it needs to be done."

HER ITEMS FIT INTO several small bags, and we donated the clothing that didn't hold sentimental value to Papa or I to Brook-Haven for those who didn't have families who cared for them. I couldn't bear to look at her writings and drawings and put them aside until after the funeral.

The funeral itself was a small affair. Whilst she was well known, it was frowned upon in the community, particularly in the newly created Section we found ourselves allocated to in GreyBrook, by virtue of where we lived - Pius was a humble, righteous section, focused on religious faith and health, and piousness. Suicide was frowned upon by the holy book on which GreyBrook was founded, but the area had been chosen for Pius because of the higher percentage of heavily religious folk in the area.

It was merely through the forethought of those who cared for her, her friends and some of her work colleagues that there was not a protest when we buried her in the central cemetery. They surrounded the small funeral party as we approached the cemetery and held back anyone who was going to force the issue.

As we were leaving, a man in a dark overcoat approached me, touching my arm to gently pull me away from Cormac, who had Rachel in the stroller in front of him.

"Isabella, it's Sennon Mathias." I frowned, until he continued, "The coroner's assistant."

"Yes?"

"It wasn't suicide," My hand flew to my mouth to stifle a gasp, "She was found... hanging in her cell, but she was deceased before she was hung up there."

"How do you know that?"

"There are a few specific things that happen when someone hangs themselves - and there are no signs of these. Oh, and the presence of an overdose amount of a medication she wasn't even prescribed."

"Why didn't the coroner say anything? He said it was a suicide," Sennon nodded,

"We had a visit from Ellwood Marshall, it was advised that it be ruled a suicide. Having been lied to myself, when my parent died, I agreed not to tell you without meaning it. So, I've just lost my job... but it felt right to do it. I'm sorry for your loss, but I felt you needed to know." I thanked him, and shook his hand, letting him go on his way.

My mother was murdered? Was there really something threatening in the visions she'd written? I had to find out now.

CHAPTER 7

The revelation by the coroner's assistant forced me to investigate the writings, and journals she'd kept while in BrookHaven, and read the Book of Prophecies from cover to cover to understand what she was trying to say. The book started as though she knew exactly who would come to be the hero she seemed to think GreyBrook needed.

"She will wear black, defiant, strong, a born leader, yet, in the beginning she will not realise. An army, small but powerful, will stand behind her, ready to fight for what is good, what is just, what is fair. She will not realise it, but she would be the best thing be the strongest thing they could hope for, the best thing that could have happened. She would be small, but mighty."

But who was she? Reading further into it, Mama had been shown the life of this young hero, but not given a name or anything that would completely identify her from birth as the hero. She had to discover that for herself, and according to what Mama had written, she may not realise in time. If she didn't, GreyBrook could become worse than Mama's visions showed it to be.

DIVIDING GREYBROOK into sections had the desired effects on the way we functioned as a city group. We were now more separate than ever divided into section based on the jobs we were required to undertake. Those with specialised knowledge, such as Cormac's friend and his engineering knowledge, could cross borders without being held up. Or, at least if they were men, or women with knowledge of the workings of childbirth - the only thing about women that the men seemed to be a little lost about and be willing to admit to. I was now being trained properly in healthcare, for when I returned when Rachel was old enough, unless I had another child in quick succession - then

I was to remain a stay-at-home mother, even though my knowledge was more electronic, and communications. Mama had always laughed that I was what they would have termed a geek on the Outside, and she didn't know how to turn the radio on without help.

"If I hadn't been pregnant with you when we came in here, and never let you leave my side, I'd not believe you came from me!" She had always muttered when I showed her yet again what to do with some new appliance.

Health care was almost beyond what I could manage. I was always a little squeamish, and now had to deal with anything that was thrown my way - blood, vomit, urine. Because of living in the area that was now Pius. However, if I had been in Luculentus, the area where they were given the electronics, and communications responsibilities, nothing would be different. It was well known to GreyBrook residents that women weren't knowledgeable enough to be trusted with the equipment that the residents of Luculentus were tasked with dealing with. Little did they realise that half the men in Luculentus were at the same stage as my mother - the gain in technology was too far advanced for them to keep up with at their ages. Cormac had a few friends who had transferred, or been transferred into Luculentus because of their mathematical prowess, who were struggling with things I would have found a piece of cake.

Chuckling, he stabbed at the new appliance we had purchased, before giving over to the one who knew how to work it, "ISA! I can at least say I tried, but this is ridiculous, how the hell do I make it work?"

A few fiddles with the cords, a tap of a couple of buttons, and a smirk later, "Tah dah!"

"You're... that's...." He paused, grinned, and continued, "Thanks!"

"I won't tell the boys, if that's what you're worried about!"

PAPA WAS TO STAY IN Pius and learn a new trade, as he had been approaching retirement age. His family were also in Pius, but had become much more standoffish since Mama had been placed in BrookHaven, and more so since her death. I knew it was hard on him, but not how hard it had become to live here, in the home he had shared with my mother.

"Isa, I've made a decision," He blurted out one day, whilst visiting for dinner

"About?"

"Staying in Pius."

"I don't understand, there isn't any choice in the matter unless you are 18 and entering selection, you have to stay, Papa."

He shook his head, a small smile on his face, as he glanced at Meredith who had also joined us for dinner, "There is another option, and it's not as bad as people make it out to be."

I frowned, then gasped as I realised what he meant, "You mean becoming Non-Sel?" He nodded, "By choice, Papa?"

"Yes, by choice. I cannot, in good conscience, live by the laws in GreyBrook as they stand, and they will not be changing in my lifetime. They are unjust, unfair, and punish victims of crime instead of criminals, and I cannot stomach it for much longer. They covered up your mother's murder, by making it look like a suicide, because she was a threat, because she knew what they were aiming to do. I tried to stay, for her. She would not leave without warning others, and when she heard about the Sections, it was too late to get her out of BrookHaven to be Non-Sel from the start." I pondered what he was saying, wondering if I pleaded with him if he would stay, but would that even be fair to him?

I was still thinking on what he had said when Meredith spoke up,

"And, I'm going too, Isa."

I lifted my head in shock, my eyes darting between the two of them, trying to wrap my head around the fact I was about to lose my best friend and my father at the same time.

"Why, Mere?"

She allowed a sad smile to wrinkle the fine scars over her face, "For many of the same reasons as your father here. I can't walk down the street anymore without being stared at, and I have to walk past him in the street, more than once when I come here. I just... I'm tired of being reminded what happened, and that I cannot do anything about it. He will always walk free, to do this to other women. To ruin other women's lives, plague them with memories they have no hope of seeing justice for the infliction of. I just can't do it anymore." I nodded. That was as close to her ever saying she had been sexually abused and tortured during the time she was missing as she had ever come, bound by the laws to never mention it under threat of jail or death, and her family being GreyBrook royalty.

"I... can't say I don't understand. I do, I really do. For both of you. But I can't, we can't. Rachel is too little, Cormac..."

"Probably wouldn't go at this point," he answered for himself, from beside me, "But I kind of understand some of it. I'm not sure I agree with Meredith, on the infliction on other women, I believe you have been harmed."

I spun on him, "What do you mean, about the infliction on other women?"

"Well, it's like they say, why were they in that area? Why were they without an escort? Wearing shorter skirts? Low cut tops,"

I clenched my hands on the tablecloth, as I stared at him, feeling the anger radiate from Meredith "Did I ever tell you about when I met Meredith? Why I always have a knife hidden on my person?" He shook his head, confused as to why I was so angry, "Remember that day, that they broadcast that there would be punishment for those two women who spoke out about being assaulted? How the crowds became emboldened, or deathly afraid? I met Meredith as we were forced to walk in a huge group of women trying to protect each other from the men determined to take what they felt was rightfully theirs to take. I had literally just 'come of age' and was fresh meat. You know where were my parents have always lived, how far away from the central broadcast that is? The group had thinned out, and they could see Meredith and I. We were forced to run for our lives to get to the house before the men caught up with us."

"Why?" Oh my, was my husband this naïve of what it was like for women here?

"Because had they caught either of them, I had no control over stopping them taking what they wanted. Isabella was of age and unmarried, so there was no husband to ask permission from, and as her father I no longer had rights over her from other men. Meredith is slightly older than Isabella, and unmarried, so would have also met the same fate." My father muttered,

"What fate?"

"Jesus, Cormac, are you blind?"

"I'm trying to figure it out, Isabella. What you are saying is different to what they taught us."

I sighed, before continuing "Cormac, they would have been well within their rights to take us and force themselves on us sexually. As and when they wished. And, believe me, you could see it in their eyes that day - they would not be kind. It had NOTHING to do with what we were wearing, why we were out there, and everything to do with the fact they had power over us, and we were female - we have little to no rights here in GreyBrook, and never have had. You probably don't notice because it doesn't affect you, and you aren't the type of guy to force yourself on anyone. But... then you said what you said just before, about not believing the other women, and hell, it sounded a little like you barely believed Meredith. You don't believe it, because you don't see it. But now, we're putting in front of you - are either of us the 'type' of women they taught you about? Is Rachel likely to be? Because as she gets older, this is her world too."

"Fuck..." He breathed, clearly shocked.

"Father, Meredith, I understand entirely why you need to go. I would join you if Rachel was older, and Cormac would come, but I will continue Mama's work in here. I will keep an eye out for the hero she foretold. I will miss you terribly."

NON-SELS WERE THOSE who refused to remain in their Section. The name having come about through the introduction of "Selection Day" for those of age to decide on where they would live and work for the rest of their lives. There was no provision for changing your mind, and those who did not choose would be expelled from the city. It was supposed to shame those who would not choose into choosing a section, lest they be associated with those who lived outside the inner gates to GreyBrook. It was supposed to be a hard life out there, none of the amenities we had inside the inner gates, no electricity, no heating, no easy access to the necessities of living. Papa and Meredith were willing to give all of that up, just to escape the tyranny that was becoming Ellwood Marshall's GreyBrook.

And, I couldn't say I blamed them.

BECAUSE OF THE CHOICE they were making, there was quite the show of disgust as they readied themselves to leave the safety of the inner gates. For something they wanted to discourage, the choice of the Section Leaders to attend their leaving was a little unusual, but soon became clear. They would make a big deal of the group leaving first, to discourage anyone else from doing so.

Papa had the original copy of the Book of Prophecies, with Mama's scribbled notes in the margins, tucked into his bag of belongings. Meredith, her own copy. I felt just slightly proud that it would not have to remain hidden out there, that they could speak about it, read it in public, and have the information out there. I was just sad that Mama hadn't been alive to see it go free.

DESPITE THE SHOUTING, and booing, Papa and Meredith stood with their heads held high amongst several others making the same decision, barely moving as Ellwood and the Section Leaders made their feelings on their choice clear to the crowd that had gathered. Papa winked at me at one point. I knew then he was very comfortable with his decision, and that I had nothing to worry about. He and Meredith would be fine and much safer together. I watched Meredith's face change as the time came to walk through the gate. Changing from a scared, troubled young woman, into a strong, confident woman. I knew more than she had ever let on about what happened to anyone else through several quiet, whispered conversations. She was hurting, needing to talk to heal, and was denied that right here in GreyBrook. We were both hoping it would be different as a Non-Sel.

They both turned slightly as they walked through the gate with the rest of the group, searching out Rachel and I, giving us a wave and smile as they walked away from us. A hard lump in my throat refused to move, as I tried to swallow my tears.

We weren't supposed to have any feelings for those who left. To feel for them was to support them, and the reasons they were leaving. Basically, making us anti-GreyBrook by needing to grieve the loss of friends and family to the 'dark side.' They thought it would discourage us from trying to join them, by making out they were evil, and anti-GreyBrook, anti-those of us left behind. For some, it did the trick, shunning those who dared to grieve the loss of a family member to Non-Sel status. For me, I chose to hide my true feelings, shoving my stroppy, unhappy feelings towards GreyBrook under the persona I portrayed: to fester for long periods.

Which wasn't the best idea they'd ever had.

CHAPTER 8

Whilst I knew I'd never be able to join my father, or Meredith, I made friends with a couple of the inner gate guards from Ferox, the new Security section. Every few weeks I could pass a letter to one of them, who would undertake what they had termed "Fence Duty", to pass to my father when they came upon either of them.

The Non-Sels had taken up residence a long way out from the inner city GreyBrook - what I discovered they termed "GreyBrook Proper" both inside and outside the Inner Gates. Somewhere under the hard facade that the leader of GreyBrook held up to the public, they had found a caring heart - perhaps not in all of them, but one who was able to get through to Ellwood Marshall, and provide health care and assistance to those who had become Non-Sel. Those on Fence Duty were to check on the health and report back, and they would send a Pius healer out to deal with anything that was required. Initially I thought it was quite altruistic of the leaders of GreyBrook after they had denounced those who had left. My father put me right.

HIS LETTERS COULD COME through unread, as those on Fence Duty who knew him well enough to give him the letters disobeyed the *"everything from Non-Sel's must be audited if coming back through the gate"* - made to stop the dissemination of information like that which was in the Book of Prophecies, or the "Black Book" as I had started to mutter.

"Isa, I know you like to think the best of people, that it helps you make sense of the world, make it feel less restrictive and hateful. I know it looks like a thoughtful thing for those high in GreyBrook Proper to have done for us. But it's not all for the safety or health of us Non-Sels, or... Without Section... as we prefer. It's all about

keeping any illness away from GreyBrook, away from the 'precious' Marshall family, and the handpicked leaders of the Sections."

I couldn't really fault that, as it would also keep Rachel and I safe, as I continued to read it.

"Those out here who get sick, they take them away, under the guise of 'taking them to the hospital for care.' But, from all reports, they are never seen again. It's easy to kill us off than spend money on dissenters who are the opposite of the 'perfect people' you want for your city. It's not the same, nor anything of the same extent, but if it had been on the Outside, it would be much like The Great Purge, an awful genocidal cleansing we vowed never to repeat. I know it's not something you will remember or have ever learned about, but it was, when it came down to it, basically getting rid of anyone who disagreed with the government, through whatever means necessary including nefarious ones.

But I don't mean to keep waffling on about the bad stuff. We're happy out here, Meredith is healthy, happier than I've seen her. I'm keeping an eye on her, I promise. I know how much she means to you.

Keep up the good fight, my love. Your mother had the right idea, even if her methods were a little... different. There are more, hidden. You will need to keep looking. And keep an eye out for our young hero.

Give little Rachel a hug from Grandpapa and stay safe.

Papa"

Folding the letter gently, I slipped it into a hidden pocket I'd sown in my jacket, and looked over at Rachel, now a pre-schooler. Papa had missed so much of her growing up. So much of all of us growing up. Whilst I still could not find out who had killed Mama in BrookHaven, I had discovered more about why they would have done it.

MAMA WASN'T MAD, NOT in the slightest. Just lost in a world of visions she had no control over. They had tried to diagnose her with what they liked to term schizophrenia, because they felt she was responding to voices, and visions that no one else could hear. On the surface, this made sense, and could easily have explained why she could have taken her life, if that was the case. But knowing she hadn't taken her own life, that someone had taken it before she was hung from the ceiling joists with a rope to make it look like a suicide, had made me look closer at what she had been writing in relation to her visions just prior to her death.

In the months prior to her death, the visions she had had were not always about the Hero we were to keep our eye out for, but about the more unusual comings and goings of the city of GreyBrook. Unusual in that they didn't happen often, if they happened at all, and Mama had dated her writing as though they were before they had happened. One or two of the notes had someone else's handwriting on them, initially rubbishing her writing, and apparent visions, then in the same handwriting, threatening her if she continued. When I had investigated the timing, and what I thought she was getting at - she had been accurate in her visions. Perhaps someone found this threatening, that something about them would soon come to the surface, and be looked down upon? Perhaps they felt they needed to shut her up? I still had no idea who, but would never stop looking, and never stopped reading through her writings, and the book.

"They will not stay silent for as long as it is wished. There will be more who stand to confront those who harm them. They will not be understood. They will be punished. But they must not stop. She, when she comes, will force them to stand, and stand they must!"

It confused me - most who remembered the punishment all those years ago knew what the outcome of complaining you'd been harmed would be and just carried on with life, not causing a stir. Who would stand up after that?

I DIDN'T HAVE LONG to wait. There had been a spate of women disappearing for a couple of nights and returning, but acting differently, all over Grey-Brook. We only knew because of a small announcement asking anyone who's loved one was missing to alert the Section Leader. A few weeks after this, there was an uproar throughout GreyBrook when Ellwood announced that yet another woman had complained about a man taking his God, and GreyBrook given right to what he wanted from her. Phrasing his announcements just right to cause those of this mind to rise into a blood lust, yet again.

Ewan Marshall had found us and warned us that Ellwood was planning an announcement, and to stay safe, "Isabella, I know that something of this sort happened to Meredith, and she felt too scared to speak of it. For the very reason that I warn you - Ellwood is mad with power and will not listen to reason. I'm sorry I could not be there, until it was too late for my daughter, but I can warn you. He knows what he is doing, when he speaks to the crowd, and wishes to incite the type of violence you will encounter. PLEASE stay safe. Keep little Rachel safe." He left in a hurry, trying to get back in time to fool Ellwood into believe that he hadn't left the Confederate Circle.

"You are all required to be present again, at the Central Billboard in your area, at 12noon tomorrow. All of GreyBrook must bear witness to what will become of you if you rebel against that which is law, that which it pre-ordained. Non-attendance will be punishable by similar methods. The men will learn something, and women - you WILL learn your place. That is all."

I sighed, this was getting ridiculous, but as a good GreyBrook citizen I organised to attend the display of punishment. Rachel was at creche, as I was supposed to be working. Those caring for others were exempt, as they could not leave them to get to the Billboard. I knew she'd be safe with her creche carer.

ELLWOOD WAS PARTICULARLY vicious this time. The woman, somewhat younger than I, not much past her 'coming of age', was stripped from the waist up, chained to the wall. She was almost too young to have been forced to see the last punishment. She literally may not have known you couldn't trust GreyBrook for its just laws, or city leaders.

I was torn between feeling sorry for her, that she hadn't picked up on the way GreyBrook functioned by now if that was the case, but also a weird sense of pride - that she would not take the injustices lying down. Realising I sounded a lot like my mother, I quickly smothered a smirk.

Watching, my guilt at feeling pride in her stand grew, as the beating continued. He wasn't easing up even though her knees had buckled, and she was lying face down, semi-conscious on the ground. Several people around me realised at the same time I did he would not stop until he killed her, judging by the stifled gasps. Being so far away from the actual beating and being able to do nothing about it tore at me, in a way I'd never felt before. I wanted to pick her up and run away with her, get her as far away from this damn place as I could. She'd been hurt by someone awful, and now the Grand Leader of our city, someone we were supposed to look up to was about to beat her to death for mentioning it. There was something so wrong about it, I physically ached.

I tried to turn away, I couldn't watch this happening with no way of stopping it. But, at the same time I couldn't do it, I had to witness this. Honour her life, her courage, and witness the atrocities this city was willing to inflict upon its residents. Tears streaming down my face for a woman I did not know, but would now never forget, I stood and honoured her in the only way I had available to me.

AFTER A TIME, IT WAS clear to those watching she was dead. We watched as it suddenly occurred to Ellwood to stop the beating. Turning to the camera, his face shiny with sweat, beads dripping from his nose, flaming red cheeks., breathing hard as he spoke.

"Take this as your final warning. Obey the laws of the Lord, and of Grey-Brook or suffer the consequences." His glare, cold and unfeeling eyes staring at the citizens of GreyBrook, was the last thing we saw before the billboard switched off.

THE BEATING, AND DEATH of the unfortunate woman did not stir up the same chaos as previous punishments had. Ellwood, having worn himself out beating a woman to death didn't have the energy to incite the same frenzy he did with the last punishment a few years ago. The crowd disperse quietly, everyone a little shell-shocked at what they had just witnessed. I joined them, plodding slowly along the path towards my work, lost in my thoughts.

Passing by an alleyway, I caught a slight flash beside me; I brushed off as a trick of the light, and continued, lost in my thoughts. Until I was grabbed roughly by the arm, and pulled off my feet, dragged backwards into the darkened alleyway. I was too startled to panic. A rough hand over my mouth and nose, preventing me from breathing, let alone screaming. I tried to plant my feet to slow down whoever was dragging me backwards. My hands clawing at their arm, raking my nails down the skin, drawing blood, and a curse from the masculine sounding person behind me. I was getting further and further away from the entrance to the alleyway, my vision fading as his hand remained clamped over my mouth and nose so tight I couldn't move my mouth to even consider biting him to get him to let go. It suddenly occurred to me he'd done this many times before, he knew what he was doing.

As my vision started to close in, I blinked as a figure seemed to rush towards me, unsure whether I should use my last breaths to panic that someone was about to join this thug in whatever he was planning to do to me, or be relieved. My body finally stopped fighting for another breath, as I saw a fist raised towards the person holding me. The last thing I registered before I lost consciousness completely was the distinct sound of a bony hand connecting with a cheek, the cheek's owner grunting in pain, and letting me go to defend himself.

I came to on the ground, watching the two of them tussle. Startled, I realised that my saviour was familiar, and grunting some terse words.

"Keep... your.... filthy.... fucking.... hands.... off my.... wife." He grunted, between traded blows. Cormac had said he would come and find me at the Billboard, but it had been too crowded, so I'd watched alone. He had apparently come looking for me afterwards. I was struggling to draw in enough air to clear my head completely and couldn't get myself upright just yet. There was a suddenly pained grunt, and Cormac fell to the ground unconscious from a serious right hook. The thug who had hit him turned to face me, smirking when he saw I was conscious.

"Ah, well, he'll get to watch if he wakes up in time." He sneered leaning over me, as I tried to back away, "He will not save you this time, damsel."

I glared at him, shuffling back as far as I could get away from him as he reached to stroke my face. He laughed, and grabbed me by the throat, dragging me up the wall, pulling on my trousers as he did so with the other hand. Struggling against his weight, I scratched at his hands, my vision darkening again as he squeezed tighter, then released his grip around my throat just slightly, as though he wanted me conscious and fully aware of what he was about to do. I would fight until my last breath, if I thought it would get me away from him, and back to Cormac, back to Rachel. Rachel! I couldn't fight until my last breath, she needed me. I needed to figure out how to get away from him, without losing my life in the process, without letting him do what he wanted without fighting back. Cormac groaned near me, as the thug got my trousers undone, thrusting his hand down them. I bit back tears, and shoved at him, raking my nails down his face, as I flailed against it with the other hand. His hand around my throat tightened, until unconsciousness threatened again. This time, I let it. I didn't want to be here for any of this, and if giving into the darkness meant I got back to Rachel alive, but damaged, then I could manage that.

SOMETIME LATER, I CAME to coughing, my throat raw, bruised. My hair being stroked by someone. I startled, and began to shove myself away from them, panicked.

"Isa, it's me. It's okay." Cormac's voice murmured from above me, as though muffled through swollen lips. I rolled my head to look up at the bruised and beaten face of my husband, "I'm sorry I couldn't stop him." I shook my head.

"Not... your... fault." I croaked, trying to sit up, rubbing my throat. I didn't hurt as much as I had expected to when I got sitting up, "Did... you... scare... him... off?"

"I came to, just as you passed out from his hand around your throat. He... couldn't hold you up, and I beat on him again," His face softened, as he looked at me, knowing what I was asking without me having to say it, "Whatever he had done before you passed out was all he did, love." My face was suddenly wet with tears I hadn't realised were waiting to be shed. My body racked with sobs, rasping harsh breaths over my damaged throat. I couldn't tell if my tears were from relief or shame. Cormac moved over to me, and gently took me in his arms, silently holding me as I sobbed, until I could draw a breath and speak.

"I'm okay, love." I murmured, my throat still burning, "I need to get away from here though." Standing up, I helped him from the ground as he grunted through the pain in his ribs to get himself upright.

"Adrenaline really has a lot to answer for," He muttered, clutching his ribs, "It didn't hurt this much when I stood up to beat the snot out of the little bastard." A very brief chuckle escaped his lips before he grimaced and cut it short.

I smiled at him, sadness at the predicament we had found ourselves in tugging at the corner of my lips as we limped our way out of the alleyway. Grey-Brook was a city that prided itself on being able to turn the other way when something wasn't right, but not anyone's business. Those we passed in the street gave small smiles, and averted their eyes from the both of us, their eyes flicking quickly over both of our injuries.

"She put up a fight, son?" Chuckled an older man as he walked past, "I see you put her in her place!" A fire I'd never seen was ignited in Cormac's eyes suddenly, a flash of movement as he decked the guy with a right hook and leaned over his startled body on the sidewalk.

"Shut your filthy mouth, pig. I would never harm my wife, nor would I ever be proud enough to brag about it. I feel sorry for your wife." He spat on his startled face, standing up and taking my hand as we walked slowly back towards our workplaces, as we would be fired if we were not to return for the rest of what was left of a shift, even with what we had just been through. I squeezed his hand as we walked together, smiling up at him, the words of my mother echoing in my ears.

"If you find one who can respect you, and fight for you, keep him."

A smile played over my lips, as I murmured to myself

"I think I did good, Mama."

CHAPTER 9

I tried to put the incident out of my mind, unable to speak of it to anyone for fear of being arrested and punished in the same way the woman whose death was now indelibly etched on my memory was. I could have fooled myself into thinking I was okay; it hadn't been that bad; he hadn't done anything. But the tight grasp of panic in my chest when I passed a random person in the street who looked a little like him, or the thudding of my heart when I was approached from behind by people I knew told me otherwise. My heart hurt for Meredith, who had endured so much, and been shunned by her parents so they got to keep the facade of normality in place. I hoped that she was happy as a Non-Sel, supported by more than just my father.

Our visits at the gate, and letter swaps, were few and far between now. My life had moved along, and I was busy raising Rachel, and expecting another. But from time to time, I would venture out to the gate to see if there was a letter or a note to say they were coming to the gate for a visit.

"Isabella, how are you? And you Miss Rachel?" the guard at our last visit had been an old school friend.

"Good, Mr Holgate. You?" Rachel had answered, "Do you have a letter for us?" He had smiled and handed over a letter from Meredith, our first update in sometime.

BACK AT THE HOUSE, I sat at the table to read what Meredith had to say, my hand resting lightly on my bulging belly.

"*Dear Isa, I hope this letter finds you well. I miss you terribly and wish there was some way I could come and see you. Particularly with the news I bring you today. I'm sorry that I could not be there to tell you what I need to tell you in person.*

This letter brings with it both good and bad news from out here in Outer Grey-Brook. It would feel wrong to begin with the good news, knowing what the bad news is, so please forgive me for starting my letter with such news.

Isabella, I have to tell you that your Papa, Everett Scott, passed over to the other side. He grew ill, and whilst the Ferox members tasked with Fence Duty tried their best to help him, your Papa succumbed to his illness after several weeks fighting it. I'm so sorry that no one could get to you, and that you could not have visited the camp. I can tell you, he was at peace, and he was comfortable. I was with him, and he wanted me to tell you he loves you and was exceptionally proud of the woman you have become. I'm so sorry, Isa."

Rachel had come into the living room to find me with my hand over my mouth, tears streaming down my face, "Mama? What's wrong?"

I choked back a sob, and stroked her face, "Grandpapa has died, my sweet. Meredith's letter was to tell me."

"Oh. I'm sorry Mama. Is he in Heaven now, with Nanny Merrin?" I nodded,

"Yes, he is."

She smiled, "Then, why are you sad, Mama? He's with his sweetheart again." I stared at my daughter in awe, when had she grown into such a thoughtful young lady? Where was my little mucky toddler?

"You're right, Rachel. He is. Thank you." The smaller Scott in my belly kicked to remind me that a mucky toddler wouldn't be all that far away either.

The letter continued,

"It feels wrong to continue on a positive note, but there is a lot of news this time. I've been meaning to tell you I've met someone out here. Someone who can see past the scars on my face, and the rest of me. Past the scars that can't be seen either. Like your mother said, if you find someone who respects you for you, keep him. So, I did! I wish you could meet him, Isa. He kind of reminds me of Cormac, but in a rugged sort of way. We've been together for about six or eight months now. His name is Jeremiah Phillips, his family was from the other side of GreyBrook, but when he became Non-Sel, because of his family, he was shunned by the Non-Sels on that side - apparently, his family are a bit like mine, but the Pius side of GreyBrook and its Non-Sels are a little more forgiving. I will take his name, to get away from the Marshall line if we make it official. You Scotts have always been... feisty - I love that you kept yours!

Oh, and that's not all. We're expecting! Sometime in the next few months - it happened early in the relationship, but he stepped up and said he wasn't going anywhere. What I haven't told him though is if it's a boy, I'd like to call it Everett after your Papa. He did so much for me when we came out here and was such an influence out here with those books your Mama wrote, that it would be an honour to do that. If it's okay with you? (And Jeremiah!).

I miss you terribly, and hope you are well, and safe. Rachel must be so big by now, at school?

Love you,

Mere."

I folded the letter and put it away, a smile on my face, despite the news of the death of my father. I was happy she had been with him, so he wasn't alone as he left this life, and wouldn't be as he entered the next with Mama. Rachel's little token of wisdom had warmed my heart and eased some of the guilt I wasn't there with him when it happened, or even known he was unwell. But he was with Mama now, and that made me happy. For Meredith, it made me happier to know she had found someone and was about to be a mother. I jotted a quick note back to her to let her know I got the letter and that I would be honoured for her to use my father's name for a son. I wished her the best and hoped to hear from her soon. I couldn't tell her any more about the goings on here, as they checked the letters at the gate, and they would arrest me for trying to speak of what had happened that day. Giving it to the guard the next day, I hoped it got to her safely.

LIFE MOVED ON AS IT always does, and the sadness at my father's passing lessened. A younger Scott joined our family in a rush one chilly afternoon, so quickly I couldn't get myself to the hospital for the birth. Which, of course, in GreyBrook was not the done thing. Given there was not a doctor on site to witness the birth, I was lucky in all sense of the word that little Chloe Melissa Scott was born living. Had there been difficulties, or she was born sleeping, I would likely have been investigated for harming her. The laws around childbirth, and reproductive health had become draconian over the years from denying women the access to what I believe was termed birth control in my Mama's time, to stop them from preventing pregnancy from occurring unless they wanted it to, to outlawing any way of ending a pregnancy that was unplanned - be it through rape, or just not timed well - over the past decade. I knew too many people who had had miscarriages of much-wanted babies, who had been investigated for trying to induce a termination, when that was the last thing on their mind, adding to their grief. Yet others who carried and raised children that were conceived by force, or who they could not afford to raise. Struggling from the beginning. It was so wrong, that we were not considered able to be in charge of our own health, and childbearing, and yet if something went wrong, it was our fault, and our fault only. Gazing at my sweet Chloe, I knew her life, and that of her older sister, would not be easy, regardless of how much their father and I loved them. I just hoped that Mama's predicted hero came in time to make a difference to them.

Rachel adored being an older sister, at an age where she understood what was required and when, so I barely had to ask if I needed a clean diaper, or Chloe needed a burp. Our little Chloe had two Mama's, one of them stricter than the other, and it wasn't me!

As I watched them both sleeping one night, I thought of Meredith and Jeremiah and wondered how they were faring with their little one, possibly a little Everett, out in a world that whilst it did not have the same draconian rules, it also didn't have the same amenities that made life a little easier with a small baby.

MONTHS WENT BY BEFORE I had another letter from Meredith, both having been caught up in the raising of tiny children. Everett Jarrah Phillips had been born healthy, around the same time Chloe had arrived. They were doing well, and he was the light of their lives. Sending her congratulations on his arrival, and a small gift, I told her of Chloe's arrival and wished them all well. I had an inkling that letters would get even fewer and further between, given the busy-ness of raising children.

I was right. Many letters went unanswered over the years, but the guards who had known both of us and were friendly towards Non-Sel's would update me from time to time, so I knew she was still doing okay, as was Everett.

CORMAC AND I BUSIED ourselves in the raising of our two daughters, and our work with the sick. From time to time, I picked up the copies of the Book of Prophecies, and delivered a few to some hidden spots, checking from time to time to see if someone had picked them up - occasionally they had. I had been delivering them in the dark, hiding from sight when curfews were in place, when I was younger. But after having the children, and the experience I had had on the walk back from witnessing the death of that young woman, I grew more and more anxious about being outside. I found myself over cautious about what the girls were doing when they visited friends, and if Rachel wasn't home by dark. The sad, terrified look on Meredith's face when she had come back after being abducted, was at the forefront of my mind. She had been on her way to visit Cormac and I when it had happened - it could have happened anytime. I know it annoyed the girls, but not as much as it frustrated me. I had been a carefree young, feisty woman when that awful man took Meredith, and when the thug tried his luck with me. Now I was scared, and anxious and it pissed me off. I was never one to cower, or hold my tongue, and now I was doing both. I tried to reason with myself that I was doing it for the girls, but I couldn't even fool myself - I was scared, and it was the fault of those two people exerting a right they were given by the city we lived in, with no hope of leaving. I had to stop letting them win, because in the end, all it did was restricted what I was doing with my life. And that made me angry.

Angrier than they would ever know.

CHAPTER 10

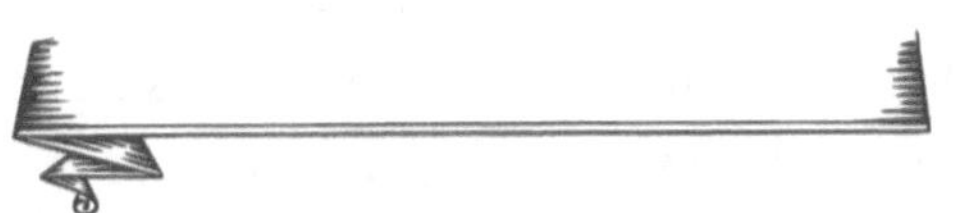

The anger I felt towards GreyBrook now, for restricting the lives of those around me spurred me into getting out there and doing something about it, albeit quietly. Starting with delivering more of the books that Mama had written and actually reading what she had written. I was startled to see that she had predicted some changes we'd had since her death, in some of her writings from her time in BrookHaven, and whilst I had believed most of what she had to say at the time, I had to admit I'd been sceptical. Now, I wasn't.

Reading through the Book of Prophecies alone at night, I was convinced that she knew what she was talking about. My hatred for the leaders of the city simmered away but was counter-balanced with an optimism that someone would come to lead us in the direction we needed to go to avoid self-implosion. Sure, I could have done something myself, but the timing wasn't yet right, there were too many unknowns as we headed into a change in governing leader.

ELLWOOD WAS GETTING very advanced in age, and in one of his more lucid moments had decided that it may be time to step down. Given his own advanced age, he had also decided that his son would be too old to begin his term as Grand Leader and had announced that he would bypass Connor Marshall and handing the position over to his grandson Barrett Marshall. Strangely, Connor was more than happy to have the reins handed to his son, rather than himself. Barrett apparently shared several of his grandfather's traits and his views - on women, on the way the city should be run, and how laws could be enforced. He was the perfect candidate to be next in line to such a position.

HE STARTED WITH A BANG. Stepped in the office of "Grand Leader of GreyBrook" at an age much younger than myself, making me feel older and older as days went by, and started laying down the law as he wished it. Starting with a random idea of outlawing black in its entirety from GreyBrook - clothing, printed material, homes. There was a bit of a struggle to print the books necessary for work and education purposes, and to purchase writing implements, until they decided that the ink in the books, and the lead in pencil were grey, not black. There was little to no explanation initially for this decision, until he introduced the "Section Colours" - now to make it obvious who was from where, and who could be questioned about being in the wrong sections, or their behaviours - Pius was known for insisting that their women were submissive, and did not hold eye contact with men for more than a few seconds, but the few women that Ferox accepted weren't held to quite these same standards.

"Also, I have been made aware of a book, a black book, of unorthodox, deviant sentiment, encouraging others to behave and belief in ways that may constitute ill-intent towards the faith and governing body of GreyBrook, has been distributed around various parts of the city. Anyone caught with this book on their person, or in their home, will be prosecuted to the fullest extent of the law available to me. This will not include beatings in the manner of my grandfather Ellwood - those will be saved for only the gravest of crimes - those which many of you have witnessed beatings for before. But it will carry a prison term, and I can assure you that our prisons are not places you want to be. All copies found will be destroyed by fire, and anyone who has information that can direct us to people with secreted copies will be richly rewarded." Barrett's announcement was thankfully made over the in-home speakers we all had to have installed when his grandfather was ruling, because the smirk on my face would have given me away immediately.

"Mama, doesn't that mean you shouldn't sneak out and deliver those books anymore?" Rachel asked, her brow furrowed.

"No, it just means I have to be even more careful when I do it, and that you have to make sure you speak to no-one about those books - or you and I both could be in serious trouble."

She nodded solemnly, then smiled, "And who would look after Dad and Chloe then? Chloe doesn't like to be dirty, and Dad doesn't know the top of the washer from the bottom." I grinned and winked at her as her father walked around the corner scowling with a twinkle in his eye.

"I could get your sister to teach me!" He spluttered, given everything she had said was true, and Chloe probably knew better at her young age than he did how to manage a washing machine. My teenage daughter was very aware of what was going around her, and never missed a thing, taking the reins in teaching her younger sister the ropes.

I WASN'T THREATENED at all by Barrett's announcement, having decided not to let GreyBrook's increasingly strict rules hold me back from what I felt was right, and what needed to be done. It made me chuckle, as it merely showed that they were scared. Scared of what the contents of the book could do, what they could stir up in the city. So, what better way to shut it down than have a book burning ritual? Mama had always said that those that forget the past were destined to repeat it and had always tried to teach me a little part of the history of Outside, and that which I didn't know was in the Book anyway. We were heading towards a repeat of a mixture of several atrocities that happened in the history before GreyBrook - book burning was a small part of a much larger atrocity that resulted in the deaths of millions of people, all because they looked different, believed different, and were thought of as less worthy. Whilst I didn't think it would be anywhere near that magnitude or even comparable, some little signs that things were going the way of the past were concerning - but only to those who knew to look out for them. Most of those people were long past, or like me, secretly taught history we weren't supposed to know so couldn't point it out to others, anyway. So, I continued to deliver the books, just less often and with much more care.

I WAS RELAXING ON A day off sorting through what books were left and trying to figure out how to get more printed, when they were now contraband that could have me arrested, when I heard Rachel come home.

"Mama, you busy?"

"In here, Rach."

"No... are you BUSY?" The way she emphasised the word was odd, making me suspicious. I threw the books back into the boxes I had around me and started to carry them upstairs.

"Ah, yes! Give me a minute." I rushed the boxes upstairs and stowed them in the furthest corner of the attic, rushing back down and grabbing the washing on my way past, making out I was folding the washing when she came into the lounge, with a friend, "Sorry! Thought Rach might have someone with her, had to get the 'smalls' put away! No one has time to see a family's smalls!" Rach and her friend giggled at the mention of 'smalls'

"Mama, this is Kahu. She's doing an exchange from Perdoctus to Pius before she reaches Selection. Can she stay tonight?" I cocked my head gently; this was the first time she had asked for a friend to stay.

"Nice to meet you, Kahu. Have you asked your homestay parents if that's okay?" She nodded; she was a very quiet young lady. We chatted quietly, while I folded. Kahu was not a name common in GreyBrook. She had laughed and told us her grandparents had heard about the creation of GreyBrook in a country a long way from where we were now, and that her name was from language native to that land. Laws against speaking of the Outside had made it so that that was all the information she had available to her, which I thought was sad, to have such a lovely name, and not be able to know its history.

Beautiful dark eyes, smooth dark olive complexion, lovely long dark black hair - she was a beautiful young lady. Which anywhere else but GreyBrook would have been a blessing, but here it could be a curse. I watched as they chatted amongst themselves, as I folded washing I had never intended to get to.

She seemed nervous but relaxed with Rachel spoke and distracted her. She startled badly when Cormac arrived home with Chloe in tow, in a happy mood, booming his arrival as he walked through the door. She backed off suddenly, frightened, trying to find somewhere small to hide. Rachel frowned at me, concern for her friend written all over her face. Cormac came around the corner, his smile changing into a grimace when he saw a teenage girl trembling in the corner.

"Chloe, did you and Dad want to cook dinner? Go on, take Dad into the kitchen and see what you can come up with?" She glanced at the girl, and shrugged, taking her father's hand and leading him away as I shrugged at him.

Rachel was still flicking her gaze between me and Kahu unsure what to do to help her friend. I moved slowly over to Kahu, who was settling, but still looking scared, and a little embarrassed.

"Kahu, it's okay. I will not hurt you. I'm just going to sit here, okay?" She nodded, barely making eye contact, as I sat down next to her on the floor, sitting quietly until she was ready to speak.

Her shoulders slumped, as she finally stopped trembling, and murmured, "Sorry, I.... just got a fright."

"That looked like more than a fright, love. Is everything all right at home? At your homestay?"

She smiled, "Yes, it's fine. It's.... not that."

She chose then to look me directly in the eye and hold my gaze for longer than normal. The pain in those eyes, that she seemed to want me to understand, made my heart pound, the anxiety I'd pushed away months ago now rising back to the surface. I knew just the smallest amount of that look personally; I'd seen in it in the mirror. But it echoed the look that Meredith had had when she returned all those years ago. Older than Kahu would have been though.

"Oh," I gave her the slightest of nods, to let her know I understood, "I see. It's okay, Kahu. Cormac would never harm you, but I understand his voice can be a little loud."

She glanced at Rachel who was pacing, trying to figure out what to do.

"What about Rachel?" She murmured, "What do I tell her? I.... made a fool of myself.... I need to explain myself."

I smiled, "In this house, we understand that there are things that never get mentioned outside these walls - things that would get anyone into trouble for mentioning it. Punished severely even. If you want to tell her, it's okay, she will tell no one. That I can promise." Kahu watched my face for a moment, trying to judge if I was lying.

"How... how did you know?"

I gave her a sympathetic look, "I've seen that look before, on a close friend of mine who is now a Non-Sel," I paused, watching her, "And I've seen a small amount of that same look in the mirror." I stood and reached out my hand to help her up, leaving her and Rachel to talk while I helped Cormac and Chloe with dinner. Cormac glanced at me, with a slight furrow to his brow as I walked in, a questioning look in his eyes.

"Not your fault, love. Just startled her." He nodded and went back to being instructed by our younger daughter on the proper way to cut carrots.

RACHEL STAYED FRIENDS with Kahu through her stay and was a little upset to find that her friend had been unwell when it came to Selection, so had missed this year. Rachel had chosen to stay in her 'birth' section and was about to enter training for the Pius way of life, serving others, being humble and submissive. She knew through having us as her parents it didn't have to be all submission, and I was confident she would find someone like Cormac who was willing to forgo the rules in the home. I'd have something to say if he didn't. She remained living at home with us, until she found that person, as the law dictated now.

Kahu joined Pius the following year, having kept in contact with us the whole time. It was clear that even her parents had no idea what she had been through, and whilst they loved and supported her, she just wanted to get away from Perdoctus, and figured that Pius would be the safest bet.

Little did she know the year we'd had in her absence.

CHAPTER 11

In the time following the end of Kahu's exchange to Pius, life suddenly got a little more difficult for us, with the laws around the book being enforced with increased vigour.

I was out early evening, visiting others and delivering the contraband book to areas I knew it would disappear, either into the hands of those who wished to read it, or those who wished to destroy it. I'd just snuck down a quiet street into a building that had been abandoned for several years now, almost derelict. I was sneaking back out, my backpack over my shoulder when I heard them.

"Ma'am! Stop right there." Knowing better than to even attempt to question the Ferox Security, once I could see who they were, I stood rooted to the spot, waiting for them to reach me. They were both young men, a little older than my own Rachel, so would have been in the positions perhaps a year. It looked like the year had hardened them.

"Evening officers. How can I help you this evening?"

"What were you doing in this abandoned building, Ma'am?"

I had to think quick and hated lying because I was awful at it, "Ah, I thought I heard someone on my walk home from work. They sounded sad, so I went to look to see if I could help." The shorter of the two didn't look like he believed a word I said. I wasn't surprised, I wasn't convinced either.

"And did you find them?"

"No, sir. I think I may have been hearing things." I shrugged and smiled sweetly at them, hoping playing the silly older lady would help.

"Still shouldn't be out here at this time of night, in an abandoned building. I will need you to hand over your bag for inspection." I swallowed. I still had a couple of books to drop off, "Is there anything in your bag we should be warned about? Needles, sharp objects and the like?"

"Err, no. Nothing other than my wallet, and spare.... sanitary products." The little short one snorted with laughter at the mention of sanitary products, as though menstruation was funny. God, how old were these two?

"Maddox, you dick. It's just a period. Jesus." The taller one was obviously a little older, but I wouldn't have thought by much. He reached out his hand, his other hand on a nightstick tucked in his belt. I shrugged the backpack off my shoulders and held it out for him. I knew it was all over but hoped against hope they wouldn't realise what it was in my bag, and I could get away with saying they were workbooks. He rummaged around and drew one of the copies out peering at it in the growing dark. Holding my breath, unable to physically cross my fingers for fear of giving away I had something to hide, I watched as he turned it over in his hands. His eyes growing wide, flicking through the pages, as he realised what he held in his hand. And I had two in there.

"Maddox, handcuff her. Ma'am, you are under arrest for the possession of not one, but two items of contraband, that could see you imprisoned for a serious length of time. You will be escorted to the cells for the night and be formally charged in the morning. You are entitled to speak, but anything you do say may be held against you." I placed my hands behind my back, not fighting them at all.

They were at least reasonably gentle as they led me to the waiting cells in Pius.

"Ma'am, is there anything you wish to say in your defence?"

"I was bringing them to you for destruction in the morning?" I tried. He frowned, a flash of belief racing across his face before doubt chased it away again.

"Then why did you not present them as soon as we approached you?"

"Because they were in my bag, and I feared you may think I was trying to draw a weapon from my bag, and harm or arrest me."

He snorted in derision, "You? Harm us with something? Ha, I'd like to see that. Women are the weaker sex. There is a reason there are almost none in Ferox - they aren't strong enough. And you? An old Pius woman harming us?" He doubled over laughing at this point.

I waited patiently for him to stop, standing at the edge of the cell with him on the other side, "I don't know why you're laughing. You all seem awfully threatened by the contents of a book. Words are less likely to harm you, than I am." I uttered, loud enough I knew both he and Maddox heard it. He slammed his hand on the bars and stormed off. Maddox eyed me with suspicion but left as well turning out the light.

LATER THAT EVENING, they brought Cormac to the cells. Apparently, harbouring someone who had read the book was a minor crime. He winked at me as he was placed in the cells next to me. After the guard I'd embarrassed and Maddox left for the night, we met at the bars.

"Well, this isn't exactly what I had planned for the evening," He chuckled, "but it could be interesting."

"The girls?"

"They're fine. Rachel will look after Chloe until we get out of here, and it's shouldn't be all that long. They've got nothing."

I hung my head, "Not true, Cormac. I still had two in my bag."

Frowning, he rubbed at his forehead, thinking, "Well, that changes things."

"So, when you get out, you will be a solo dad for a while. I doubt they'll let me out, particularly when they realise I'm directly related to the author, and that she was the 'mad' woman they detained for such writing." I looked up at him suddenly, "Shit. They will think I'm bonkers and never let me out."

"Don't think like that. We'll figure something out, I promise."

CORMAC WAS RELEASED a day later, a slap on the wrist for associating with a criminal. Thankfully, they hadn't thought to search the house, and hadn't connected the two books to there being more. We could all be in serious trouble if they ever put it together.

"Isabella Maria Scott. You have been charged with possession of illicit and damaging materials. Given you were found in possession of these items there will be no trial, as your guilt is obvious. You will spend the rest of this year in the cells, unless you tell us where the rest are."

"What rest? There was only ever the two I had. I can't tell you where any more are, because I found those separately."

He shook head, almost sadly, "Perhaps after a few weeks in solitary, you'll tell us."

They gave me a moment to talk to my husband and children, who were both looking a little shell-shocked at what was happening.

"Cormac, take good care of them. Rachel, you help your father with the things I used to do, and Chloe, you help them both okay? I will see you sooner than you think, I'm sure,"

Cormac made a face, "What do I do wit-"

I interrupted him abruptly, "The dishwasher? Rachel knows how to turn it on, and the other things - Meredith will sort them." I winked at him, out of sight of the guards.

"Ah, yes, I will talk to her. You must come home soon; we can't live on my cooking!" He gave the smallest of nods to acknowledge he understood, and kissed my cheek, "You'll be fine. I love you and will see you whenever I can."

THEY LED AWAY ME FROM the holding cells in Pius into secure transport to the bigger women's prison in Ferox, the only section properly set up for holding convicted criminals. I hadn't been found mad and hadn't been linked to Mama in BrookHaven. Nervous was an understatement. I didn't know what other kinds of women were locked up in the prison, or who I'd get roomed with. As I travelled in the transport, alone in the back, I got to thinking - I assumed that these women were hardened criminals, locked up for crimes like murder. Yet, I was now one, and all I'd done was possessed two copies of a book feared by the Grand Leader and his Section Leaders. Perhaps some of them had been murderers, or violent, but given our city, and the laws written the way they were, it was more likely they were in prison for reasons like mine - something that harmed no one, but threatened the insecurities of those in positions of power. Our laws protected only those who needed the protection from being prosecuted for crimes - those who had the power and the money to brush their crimes under the carpet and get away with it. I chuckled to myself; I wondered what Ellwood and the founders of GreyBrook had been trying to hide from when they created a city to hide their crimes within, with its governing laws basically favouring only them, and people like them. I was seriously curious to find out.

It was dark by the time I reached the prison in Ferox, led to a cell with a sleeping roommate. Lying down, staring at the roof, I tried to make peace with the fact that this would be my home for the next year at least. Thankfully, at least on that first night, my cellmate wasn't a snorer. Not that it mattered anyway, I barely slept that night, nerves about what to expect that next morning too much to settle down to sleep.

OVER THE COURSE OF the following months, I got to know more of the women in here. A few were locked up for serious offenses like murder, though the two women I spoke to with murder on their record, and an expansive stretch. Most were just as I had expected - imprisoned for minor offences in the grand scheme of things - speaking ill of both Ellwood and Barrett, speaking back, and one of them was for handing in one of the books.

"So, they arrested you as you were handing it in?"

She nodded, chewing on her breakfast before she spoke, "Well, kind of. I had just picked it up and had no idea what it was. No trial, found guilty by possession. How the hell did you have two?"

I shrugged, "I'd found a couple, had a wee read before putting them back, which is what I was trying to do that day."

"Put them back, not hand them in?"

"No, not hand them in. Like I said, I'd had a read," I looked around, leaning forward to talk to her, "What the author had to say was kind of interesting. So, I hid them in slightly different places. Or at least was trying to."

She smirked, "That'll be why you got a year and I got six months. Though, they said you were going to hand them in."

"One day maybe. They didn't ask me to be specific, just what I was doing with them. It's stupid though, they offered a reward - what is the reward in here if we were arrested and charged with possession, yet we were handing them in?"

Another lady chuckled, "A break from the kids?" All the mothers in the group laughed somewhat sadly. We all missed our children, but the break from the noise was bliss.

IT WAS PARTICULARLY hard on everyone when it was visiting day, and our children visited either on their own if they were adults.

"Mama!" called Rachel as she sat waiting, coming on her own this time, "Papa said to tell you Meredith finally got all the gifts you asked him to give her. Not that I have any idea what that was." She winked at me, as I smiled.

"How's things going Rachel? Is Papa okay?"

"He is, Mama. He and Chloe miss you in the house, but I visit when I can. I miss being able to ask you stuff without having to go through waiting for visiting times. Or being able to just come over and tell you something." Her face lit up suddenly, 'Kahu is coming to Pius when she gets selection redo soon - I can't wait!"

"I'm so happy that she got to decide. How is she doing?" I asked quietly, knowing it was illegal, and would earn me more prison time if we spoke clearly about what I was asking,

Rachel grimaced, "Her parents have some idea, but as I remember you telling me with Aunty Mere, they can't really do or say anything. She hoped that she could get away from the memories coming here. And I think she may have become friends with one of the Taylor boys whilst she was here. The slightly awkward one, that likes the religion side of Pius more than most." I frowned, trying to remember his name.

"Jeffery?"

"Yeah, that's him. They seemed happier in each other's company, but he's a little odd."

I chuckled, "Odd isn't the half of it."

Rachel shook her head as she shook with suppressed laughter, "Oh well... if they make each other happy."

"That's true. When will she arrive?"

"In a few months' time, after your sentence is over, I think." I looked up at the calendar they had in the family visit room, nodding, "I can't wait - for either of those, Mama!"

"Neither can I, love. Neither can I."

CHAPTER 12

The problem with having a criminal record in this city, particularly for what could be considered subversive actions, possessing disruptive and trouble-making literature, was that it meant I was under surveillance for the rest of my natural life as a potential threat to the stability of the great city of Grey-Brook. It also meant my family were under surveillance but to a lesser degree.

Most of a year in prison, and I was surprised at how much had changed, and not for the better. This was GreyBrook after all, it wasn't likely to get better until it benefitted those in high places. Nothing that would benefit those in higher places was likely to be of any benefit to those of us in the rest of the city. It was more likely to be detrimental than anything. Laws had become tighter, and more controlling of how the residents of GreyBrook could go about their business. I was thankful that Cormac had gotten the other books out to Meredith, as now it was difficult to get anything out of the gates, unless you were a Ferox guard, or a Ferox on fence duty, or the farmers of Arator tending to the fields between the Non-Sel camp and the inner walls.

RACHEL MOVED OUT AGAIN when I came home, having moved in to help her father and Chloe run the house. The men of GreyBrook weren't always taught the more 'feminine' jobs around the home, given the fixation of GreyBrook's founders on gender and gender roles. Cormac hadn't wanted to ask, or look like he couldn't cope, but Chloe at her young age had no qualms telling her older sister that Dad had burnt dinner several nights in a row and didn't know how to wash her school uniform properly. Rachel and her husband moved in for several months, just to 'keep Dad company", but had helped to keep the household running smoothly enough that Chloe had barely noticed I wasn't there.

A WEEK AFTER THEY RELEASED me, Kahu arrived in Pius, staying with Rachel until she found someone for herself. GreyBrook frowned on women living alone, or even in groups without a man, so the situation was frowned upon until Jeffery Taylor finally got his act together and asked for her hand in marriage. Whilst he was an odd one, he did everything traditionally, and even made the trip to visit her parents in Perdoctus to ask for her hand. From what Rachel had said he was traditional when it came to the roles within the home, and relationship, but Kahu was looking for some stability, and safety. She found that in Jeffery.

I CAME HOME FROM WORK one day, to a beaming Rachel and her husband sitting on the couch. Cormac, fixing hot drinks in the kitchen, had been surprised by them moments before I had come home.

"What's got you two all overcome with happiness?" I asked as I sat down, a hot cup of tea cupped in my hands, "Not that it's a bad thing!"

Rachel patted a fairly nervous looking Jason's hand, "Mama, Papa. We have some news."

"Do tell." Cormac murmured, a slight frown tickling his brows as he watched Jason rubbing his hands together, a wry grin nudging the edge of his lips as I watched an idea cross his face and glanced back at Rachel who was waiting for everyone to pay attention.

"Jason and I are expecting our first child in about five to six months' time." I'm not ashamed to admit I did the whole 'hands over my face in surprise, happy tears, expectant grandma' thing that is entirely expected of us, and completely out of our control. It embarrassed Rachel beyond measure, as I knew it would, but Jason took it well.

'Rachel, it's good practice. My mother will do the same thing."

"It's basically a Grandmother's rite of passage, Rach," chuckled Cormac, as Chloe flew across the room to hug her big sister, giving off a younger person's version of my behaviour, "And an aunt's"

THE PREGNANCY WENT well, Rachel and motherhood worked out better than it had with the two of us, even though we were close. My mother had been going slowly mad, so I guess there had been some strain there. Her wee girl Melissa was a happy little baby, her father's eyes, and her mother's calm temperament. Slept blissfully through Aunty Kahu and Uncle Jeffery's wedding, and only wailed when someone tried to put her down instead of dancing with her, a look of complete bliss when she was back up being danced around. Her Aunty Chloe loved doting on her, and talked often about having her own children, babysitting for her older sister whenever she was allowed, with our help.

CORMAC SURPRISED ME on our anniversary, with a small nondescript package given to me after the celebrations had been had and the house was quiet, and mostly empty aside from us, and a sleeping Chloe.

"Your Papa gave me this a long time ago, before he left to be Non-Sel."

Opening the package, I gasped - a copy of the Book of Prophecies in my mother's handwriting sat in my hands, "But... Papa had the original. They're using it in Outer GreyBrook to make copies, aren't they? Meredith didn't give it back to you?"

"He has the original, but apparently she wanted you to have one. She wanted you to have your own personal copy, with her own touches. He apparently found it in her things from BrookHaven, with a little note in it." He motioned towards the book, as he winked and left to have a shower.

I opened the book in my hand, overcome with emotion at seeing my mother's eccentric looking handwriting again, tears running down my face, swiftly wiped away with my free hand before they fell from my chin onto the book. This one had been typewritten, which was different to Papa's original, but this one was different in more than just how it was written. It contained little handwritten notes on the visions, little extras she had come up with when re-writing it for me, little notes that didn't even exist in Papa's copy of the book.

Running my fingers over the writing, I was drawn to read it again, paying more attention to it as I took in the little notes my mother had made, which may only make sense to anyone who knew her particularly at the end.

"She will wear black, defiant, strong, a born leader, yet, in the beginning she will not realise. An army, small but powerful, will stand behind her, ready to fight for what is good, what is just, what is fair. She will not realise it, but she would be the best thing be the strongest thing they could hope for, the best thing that could have happened. She would be small, but mighty." - the little note Mama had made next to it was a little confusing *"She will not arrive alone, but she will always feel alone. Different in skin, different in who she will love, always alone."* My mother had always been good at picking up on when someone wasn't right, feeling awkward in a situation, perhaps that is what she meant? Someone who was a little awkward? I knew plenty of people like that. I closed the book gently, as a little piece of paper fluttered out towards the floor.

"Everett, you make sure she gets this, no matter what. Isa, I know you'll know what to do with this. I love you both, Merrin." Smiling, I gently slid the paper back in, almost hearing her soft admonishment of my father if he hadn't given it to me. I slid it into the secret compartment Cormac had built into the wall behind our bed, and crawled into bed, overcome with exhaustion from the celebrations of the day, and the swirling thoughts in my head after reading parts of Mama's book.

I HAD TO BE PARTICULARLY careful of what I paid attention to outside of our home, what I mentioned to others outside of the family, especially as I read further and further into the book, now I had more information than I ever had before with the little footnotes. Mama yet again mentioned *'I know you'll know what do when the time comes.'* Directed at me, but I still didn't get it. I worried I wouldn't get it even when it mattered, that I'd miss the signs. I lost sleep with worry, until late one night I realised that my worry meant I believed wholeheartedly in what my mother had predicted, and if that was the case, I'd be looking out for it.

But if I paid too much attention to something, or spoke to the wrong person, I was at risk of being locked away again, this time for good. The problem with the surveillance was that I wasn't the type of person to take anything that happened that was unjust, lying down. I had always been what they had termed "mouthy" and had been in trouble because of my inability to bite my tongue for long before now. I had found a few people I recognised popping up at events I attended, and I'd had a few house calls to ensure I was not harbouring those who felt similarly to me, and not reporting them. The secret compartment in the bedroom was a godsend, for the days they felt like rummaging through the entire house looking for contraband, anything to put me back into prison. I could have complained, but in GreyBrook, who would listen? Sure, Cormac could have complained, but given he had been harbouring one who encouraged subversive behaviour, he had lost friends and respect in the circles he had been involved in. He had lost a lot to remain loyal to me, to my family, and its hopes for change.

"Why, Cormac, why do you stay? You've lost so much because of us, because of the Scott family, and this damn book. Why do you stay?" I had asked, on a day where I was feeling down about the stress I had caused the family.

"Because I believe in the cause, in what your mother had to say, and the changes that GreyBrook needs. Even if it doesn't happen in my lifetime, I believe it will happen, and I want to be a part of that for my children, and grandchildren. Our parents decided to come to GreyBrook, believing that it was the best choice for everyone at the time, and whilst we now know it may not have been, we can change it. That's why I stay." He paused, as I playfully frowned at him, "Oh... and I love you, there's that too!"

"MAMA! PAPA!" RACHEL'S voice echoed up the stairs, on a fine Saturday afternoon, "You there?"

"Coming!" I yelled back, dropping the washing I was folding on the bed, and happily leaving the job behind. Cormac followed from his study, joining me on the couch.

"You guys can come in now," Rachel murmured to whoever was hiding in the kitchen. There was a slight shuffling, as a startled Jeffery Taylor was pushed rather ungracefully into the lounge.

"Er, hello there Jeffery. Will Kahu be joining you?" I gathered she was still in the kitchen, being the 'pusher' of Jeffery into the lounge.

"She was supposed to be first! But she got a little shy, I think." He muttered, looking embarrassed.

"Kahu Taylor, come on in. No need to be shy in this house, you know that."

Footsteps sounded in the kitchen, as she chuckled, "Yeah, but wait till you see how I've let myself go," and rounded the corner, belly first.

"Oh... wow!" I breathed, as she moved into the lounge with an enormous pregnant belly, "Has it been that long since I saw you last?" More chuckling from Kahu, and now Rachel.

"No, Mama Scott. There's apparently more than one in here."

I blinked, stunned, "Really? How do they know?"

"They felt two different heads? How did they know when you were pregnant?"

"Same thing, I guess. Two is unusual though! My Mama used to say they could look with some special technology and even see whether the child would be a male or female. But... they didn't bring that technology with them." I suddenly realised the rest of the company I was in, mentioning Before and the Outside, and slapped my hand over my mouth, "Shit. Sorry."

Kahu laughed, and patted Jeffery's hand, softening his frown, "Ah, we forgive ya, you're.... old."

"You cheeky.... actually, no... that's true. I am, and judging by my family history, probably more than slightly eccentric!"

Kahu was still some ways from due, and keeping healthy, but had known that her pregnancy was high risk, and waited to tell anyone, avoiding those who might notice her growing belly as pregnancy until it was too big to hide, and she had reached a time of safety if the babies were in a hurry to arrive.

GreyBrook did not really have facilities for sickly babies or children with difficulties of any kind. It barely catered for its elderly population, the founders of the city. If you could not serve the city, the city will not serve you. However, the hospital had the highest grade of health technology possible thanks to the brains of Luculentus, to ensure that those who could continue to serve the city once recovered could recover as quickly as possible. But nothing to help you in the beginning - if you were not healthy enough to survive on your own, Grey-Brook had no need for you.

For a city that was supposed to be the greatest place on earth, how it's they treated citizens was more like inmates of a prison. But unlike prison, it was difficult to tell who the monsters were.

CHAPTER 13

The arrival of the twins was a big deal in Pius, and in GreyBrook. Live twin births were not the usual, given their high risk and GreyBrook's refusal to intervene in any difficulties of birth or the immediate aftermath after if the child or children were early. So many of the future generation were lost in the early days of illness and conditions that had they been an adult, GreyBrook would have treated. Both Taylor twins survived, and were healthy, albeit small.

I had the honour of meeting the babies early on after their birth, Kahu taking them home the day post the birth, asking quietly for help from myself and Rachel until her mother could come from Perdoctus to assist for a month. Any longer, and her mother would lose her job in Perdoctus and have to become Non-Sel - only those raising children could be away from their jobs longer and remain. Because they were raising the next generation to serve GreyBrook.

THE BABIES WERE TINY wee things, only a few days old. Small, which was apparently normal in a twin pregnancy that ended just a little early. Not a lot of room in one uterus, it seems! But still cute, and not in that 'new baby' everyone says is cute, but really are just being nice way. They were actually very cute. Darker skinned that those around them, because of Kahu's complexion, so as well being a cause of celebration being a healthy twin birth, they were also a cause of much discussion, as the first obviously biracial babies in Pius. Grey-Brook had tried to pride itself on being inclusive, but it seemed that those that held the beliefs that began the founding of the city were often of the paler complexion, and of similar religious faith. That was where the Scott family had differed, at least from my parent's generation onwards, anyway!

Kahu was a natural mother, finding her way with the babies quickly and easily. Whilst Jeffery was a little more awkward. I couldn't put my finger on it, but it seemed to be with the girl child whom they had named Reed. He seemed more comfortable with the boy child, Jameson, even though at this point aside from the obvious there was nothing different about them or how they needed to be cared for.

I ENJOYED THE TIME I spent with them, and helping Kahu, but all the while had something tickling away in my brain, something I couldn't put my finger on. But it was something to do with the babies. After a week with Kahu, Jeffery and the twins, I returned home, trying to figure out what was trying to make itself known. Muttering away to myself, I realised yet again that I sounded just like my mother.

"Oh... that could be it!" I chuckled and retrieved the book from its hiding place behind the headboard, skimming through the pages I had read already, trying to find the 'vision' I thought might have something to do with whatever it was.

Tiny from birth, she will be one of two. An unusual occurrence, the cause of many celebrations. A boy, and a girl. He will be her greatest supporter, but also her most judgemental friend. Life will not be easy, a daughter to a father who wishes to be free of the burden of a lowly girl, favouring the boy. Speaking her mind, she will find herself in strife often, risking both physical punishment, and legal.

"Am I just over thinking it?" I muttered, startled to hear Cormac reply

"Overthinking what love?"

"Holy shit, love. I didn't know you were there. I was just thinking about the babies, and something I read in Mama's book."

He smiled, that affectionate but placating smile only partners can give, "You think one of them is your Mama's hero? Already? Why?"

"No... not necessarily. Just... something about the kids is different."

"Aside from them being biracial and there being two of them?"

"Aside from that. Mama spoke of the father being different with them. Jeffery is awkward with Reed, but relaxed and casual when he cares for wee Jameson. It... was just odd."

"He's a new father, Isabella. Remember when Rachel was born? I was a mess. But with Chloe, it was easier. Jason and Rachel were the same with wee Melissa."

"Yeah, but this is at the same time. It's not like he's learnt something that makes it easier to look after Jameson because Reed came first. Even in the birth order I don't think she did!"

He shrugged, "Perhaps. But, you asked, and yes, I think you're looking too hard for something that isn't there, yet."

I CONTINUED TO READ the book, drawn to the handwritten comments, and the content again. The tickle had not left, despite Cormac's attempts to dissuade me from pursuing it. It was a day later I came upon the little comment that my mother had made and things started to click even more.

"She will not arrive alone, but she will always feel alone. Different in skin, different in who she will love, always alone."

The comment initially confused me and still did. But it was describing the wee baby I had held in my arms just days ago more and more. She did not arrive alone, and they both differed in skin. I didn't understand the part about different in who she would love and if it was her, probably wouldn't until she was older. Though, in GreyBrook, aside from the interracial marriage of Kahu and Jeffery, nothing different happened. Men married women, women married men, it was as it had always been. I frowned, trying to remember if it had been any different, or if there had been a kerfuffle about something aside from race? Anything else bar men and women had been banned by the faith of the Founders, perhaps it was that? And currently she wasn't alone or could be lonely.

"Oh... okay, I'm overreaching." I sighed to myself and put the book away again.

KAHU AND JEFFERY RAISED the twins well, into polite, respectful children, and teenagers. Despite the trouble that began when a newish family moved to Pius in a rare change of Section post Selection, which saw Kahu become withdrawn and anxious, overprotective of the children. Rachel and I had watched when she had withdrawn into herself whilst we were out with all the children one afternoon, at a park and the new family walked past. Having had several conversations with the family myself, there was nothing out of the ordinary about them - the Barlow's being of a similar age to both Kahu and Rachel, and their wee son Walker a similar age, if not slightly older than the twins and Melissa. When pressed, Kahu would not talk about anything to do with them, or her withdrawal when they approached - not even to Jeffery. We learned to let it go and leave her to it. The Barlow's didn't seem to notice.

REED IN PARTICULAR used to love coming over for a chat with anyone who was here. The age difference between Melissa and the twins was just that little bit too big for them to grow up as friends, but they got on well as Melissa was often over when Reed came for a chat. Rachel had come to help as I aged, particularly after Cormac had been tragically taken in a worksite accident, tending to some injured after a new building collapsed, and the site had not been secured properly before the Pius emergency crews were sent in to assist the injured.

Melissa often joked that Reed was a little odd, but not in the same way that Jeffery was odd, often to Reed's face. To her credit she just laughed, and agreed that her father was a little strange, but that she was just thankful she wasn't that strange. She particularly enjoyed the stories that my children and grandchildren had gotten sick of, the stories of before. Stories that my mother had passed to me, and insisted I pass on to Rachel, who had insisted I tell the stories to Melissa who wasn't all that interested. Luckily, Reed was.

SOMETIMES WEE REED reminded me of myself in the early days, just a little pissed off with the world, all the fire in her belly she needed to do something, but nothing she could change. Her questions regarding how it was before, and why anyone would think this was any better, let alone the best thing out used to make me chuckle much to her chagrin thinking I was laughing at her. She seemed to come more when she was stressed about something, and I didn't mind that at all.

"How's life at home, Reed? You're here more often at the moment, which isn't a bad thing by any means, I love having you here. Just wanting to check is all."

Blushing, she had nodded, "Yeah, nothing new. Dad ignores me to concentrate on Jameson and his selection choices, and Mum tries to make it look like it's not happening, but just annoys Dad by making too much of a fuss over what I'm doing. I enjoy coming here, because you'll listen to all my silly worries about Selection and school, and the treasures I find and all that shit.... sorry... stuff."

"Oh, love, you can swear here. I've a mouth like a garbage pail when I get going - filthy!" The chuckle that came from the very serious young lady in front of me warmed my heart. I was worried about her, but the cheeky noise she made when she laughed told me underneath it all there was an inner happiness.

IT WAS AFTER THIS CONVERSATION I recalled the standout quotes in Mama's book

"*Life will not be easy, a daughter to a father who wishes to be free of the burden of a lowly girl, favouring the boy. Speaking her mind, she will find herself in strife often, risking both physical punishment, and legal.*" Grabbing the book from the hideaway, the little note from my mother fell out, her words glaringly obvious as it floated to the floor - *Isa, I know you will know what to do with it when the time comes.*

"Oh, Mama," I muttered, stretching my aching old knees, "Yes, I do."

The following day, my own copy of the Book with my mother's wavy handwriting was safely hidden in the derelict building I had been arrested in all those years ago.

I knew I could be wrong, that my mother could have just been eccentric, and demented by the end, and it could all be for nothing. That the monsters that they had built the walls to keep out wouldn't destroy us first, having been locked in here with us from the beginning. It could all be a big pipe dream.

But at least we had had some hope, and right now - that was all we had.

To Be Continued...

Continue The Alexis Chronicles in the next novel, She Wore Black.
http://www.jlparkauthor.com/shop/

About the Author

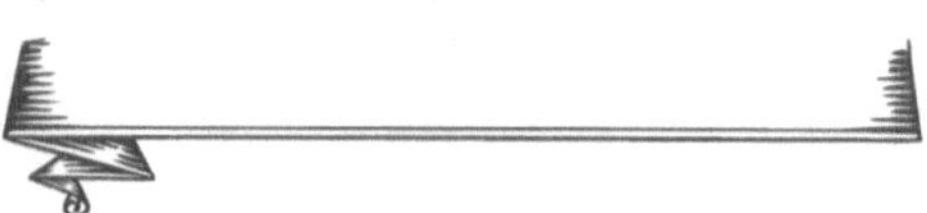

J L Park is a mother of 2, from beautiful New Zealand/Aotearoa in the Southern Hemisphere, who always has too much to do, and not enough time – but will always find time for two things – her family and her writing

When she's not working, or studying, as an RN, she can be found playing with her wife and children in the sun or immersed in the worlds of her writing. Learn more about her at jlparkauthor.com[1].

https://www.facebook.com/jlparkauthor

https://www.instagram.com/jlparkauthor

https://www.bookbub.com/profile/j-l-park

---

1. http://www.jlparkauthor.com